WHOODATHUNKET

And the Girls

TK Cassidy

MW01094803

Also By TK Cassidy

Whoodah Hitchins
Raven's Tale
The Life and Times of 13B
The 500 Year love
Almost Brilliant
The Distinctive Plop

New Works in Progress/Upcoming
Jericho
Winn, Luz & Draw, Detective Agency:
We're Always on Your Side

Copyright © 2018, TK Cassidy

Cover art by Diana Sharples, 2018

All rights reserved by author. No part of this book may be used or reproduced in any manner whatsoever without written permission except in the case of brief quotations embodied in critical articles or reviews. This book is a work of fiction. Names, characters, businesses, organizations, places, events and incidents either are the product of the author's imagination or are used fictionally. Any resemblance to actual persons, living or dead, events or locales is entirely coincidental.

JSNM Ink Publishing

ISBN 9780966015225

For more information, visit the author's Amazon page: TK Cassidy Amazon Author Page

For even more information,

Visit the author's website: TKCassidyWrites.com

Author Note

This has been a fun story to write. The story was originally birthed when I saw a greeting card with three little old ladies sitting in the middle of a hectic train station. They looked to be triplets; grey haired, support hose and orthopedic shoes. Two were looking into a purse while the third stared off into space. Immediately, I saw my main characters: Niddie, the oldest and most independent; Aggie, the middle and the peace maker; and Poppet, the youngest who was always needy, always in a different place than her sisters.

The second inspiration came from my amazing aunts who made me believe that what I wanted these fictional women to do was possible. They're all in their seventies, still taking long bike trips, hiking, traveling, and all have more energy than many of the much younger people I know.

Thanks for being such awesome role models, Aunt Ethel Marie, Aunt Mary Ellen and Aunt Honey! (BTW, Poppet is NOT based on any one of these ladies!)

For the record, I did a lot of research for the sixth chapter. I have no experience with drugs and I'm fairly certain neither do my aunts. I wrote that part of the story because the tale insisted on that section being written. I beg you, dear reader, to use all the verisimilitude you have to just enjoy the story and forgive my lack of knowledge.

Acknowledgements

Writing a book might be a lonely, one-person affair, but getting one ready for release is a major collaboration. I'm grateful to have a network of people I can call on for help.

Thank you to the beta readers I count on to not only find mistakes in my nearly final copy, but to suggest changes to make the story stronger - my long-time colleague and friend, Rayda Reed; long time friend and cohort in crime, Barbara Sjostrom Treasure; new reader, Linda Sjostrom; fellow teacher and cousin with a great eye, Vikki Thune; and, last but hardly least, Ethel Marie Ellingson, one of the inspirations for this romp through insanity. You guys are amazing.

I'd also like to extend a generous gift of gratitude to my newest bff: fellow writer, confidante, partner in laughter, editor, book formatter-par-excellence and continuous motivator, Lynessa Layne. Without you, this would still be on my "one-of-these-days" pile.

Of course, the support of my wonderful husband, Dale Fleming, knows no bounds. MSB, I appreciate you more than you know. You're always the first to laugh in all the right places.

Chapter One

The three septuagenarian sisters slumped around the memory-scarred kitchen table and stared into the ancient, chipped porcelain cups they held between their trembling hands. Still spry after 30 years of librarianship and 70 plus years of life, Niddie sat at the head of the table. Despite her years, she still rode her big, brown horse, drove the rusty, faded green John Deere tractor and mucked out the few stalls they used when the need arose. Tonight, her hands shook slightly as she lifted the barely warm coffee to her lips and took a quiet sip. She'd run this little truck farm all of her adult life. Anger gathered up inside her. She was not going to be pushed off now ... she hoped.

All three women snapped their heads toward the window at the sound of a soft whoosh and the glass rattling. Niddie looked at Aggie and asked, "What was that?"

To Niddie's left, the second sister, Aggie shook her head. "Sounds kind of like an explosion somewhere closer to town, but I'm sure that's nothing to concern us. We have plenty of other things to worry about."

On the right side of the table, the youngest sister, Poppet offered. "I heard some big company's drilling around the area looking for minerals and stuff."

Niddie pursed her lips and puffed out a disgusted breath, shaking her head. "You don't know what you're talking about! There are no minerals around here of any value? They'd have been found years ago."

"Besides," Aggie interjected. "... if that was going on, the whole town would be talking and I haven't heard anything."

Smug in the knowledge that she knew something her sisters didn't, Poppet pressed her lips together and lifted her hands to chin level, pretending to look at her fingernails. Then she simpered. "Well, maybe if you two would come to bingo more often you'd know as much as I do."

Both Niddie and Aggie smirked at the idea of Poppet knowing anything about mineral drilling as well as the idea of anyone doing such a thing around here. Niddie pulled the conversation back to the topic at hand.

"Well, I don't see any way around this? Do you, Aggie?" She looked at the sister on her right, Agatha Constance. Four years younger, Aggie still worked the gardens and kept track of the vegetable plots on their 33 acres. She knew which sections needed to be left fallow, when the hay needed to be mowed and which areas could be rented out to a farmer in need for some extra grazing. Aggie's lip trembled at the idea of having to leave the only place she'd ever really called home. She shook her head as she blew unnecessarily on the tepid coffee.

"Well! I! Will! Not!" Poppet, the youngest at 71, pressed her plump arms across her ample breasts, planted her feet defiantly and fixed a stare of outraged indignation on her reddening face. "I was a nun for Heaven's sake! I will not become a ... a common criminal just to satisfy your whims." Hot chocolate slopped onto the table as she snatched up the fragile cup.

Niddie softly snickered. She turned to look at her youngest sister with a look bordering on contempt. "You were a nun trainee for two pitiful months. Then you came running home because you had to wash floors without a mop and they didn't allow televisions in the convent and ..." Niddie paused for effect. "... no Oreos." Poppet gasped. "I hardly think that qualifies you for canonization," Niddie finished.

Niddie watched her youngest sister fluff herself up indignantly. This was all part of Poppet's dance. She had to be the one who said no to everything. That way, if anything went wrong, she could get on her high horse and lord over everyone that she'd warned them not to do whatever they'd done. Her sisters knew the best way to handle Poppet was to simply sit, sip their drinks and wait out the tempest.

After ranting on for a few minutes without any response from the other two, Poppet realized her actions weren't having the desired impact on her sisters. She placed the half empty cup back on the old surface more gently and casually swiped at the spilled chocolate with a cheap paper napkin.

Upset at her sisters' lack of empathy, her deep blue eyes welled as her mopped up the spill. Then she brushed imaginary dust from her calf length black skirt and then the sleeve of her spotless white shirt as she considered the situation. From under lowered lashes, Poppet regarded her oldest sister who'd turned back to her coffee. Niddie had always been bossy, but rarely was she so cruel. Poppet pulled herself up as tall as her 4′ 11″ body would take her and threw her chin out. "Well, at least, you know how I feel!"

Niddie mostly ignored her youngest sister when she was in this mood. She knew Poppet had no idea what they were up against. Poor Poppet had remained childishly naïve all her life. She had always lived in a world of her own making. Niddie'd given up hope that that would ever change years ago.

The two older sisters sighed in unison and sipped their drinks once more. Even after all these years, when discord arose, they fell back into their childhood roles. Niddie shook her head slightly and let her eyes drift around the familiar old-fashioned kitchen. Nothing had changed in her lifetime.

Sometimes she felt like she could still see Momma standing there by the now chipped enamel sink, peeling potatoes into the very same pot she herself had used for last night's dinner. The paint on the faded white trim was peeling from the warping window frames. Through the cracked window over the sink, she could see the once bright red and faded white trim barn.

The other buildings were close to falling over. The surrounding sagging unpainted fences threatened to follow the leaning barn's example. None of the roofs on the old buildings had been replaced for more than 30 years. Every year, new leaks seemed to spring up whenever the rains came.

Niddie's unadorned, arthritic fingers rubbed the edges of the ragged, scrunched envelope hidden in her lap. The message was the warning letter from a recent visitor. That letter was what had started this whole argument.

Aggie, the peacemaker, scraped the legs of her creaky mismatched chair on the cracked once-white linoleum and went to stand behind Poppet.

"Now, now, Dearie, don't start blubbering. Niddie didn't mean to hurt your feelings."

Aggie glared at Niddie. She rubbed Poppet's shoulders as she continued to blubber into her arms. "She has a valid point, you know, Niddie. No matter how you spin what we're talking about, this is against the law."

"I know! Believe me, of all of us, I'm the one who knows. Who do you think keeps this family together?" Niddie rose quickly to her aching feet and paced the farmhouse kitchen slowly. "Well, you just tell me what the hell you want me to do? I'm open to any suggestions from any party." She strode back over to stand in front of her sisters. "Which one of you has a better idea?"

Poppet clapped her hands over her ears and turned into Aggie's comforting embrace. Niddie continued, "Do you, Aggie? You have any other plans? How about you, Poppet? Do you have a big old hidden stash of money somewhere?"

"No need for cursing, Niddie. We know we're in trouble." Aggie snatched another cheap napkin from the old dispenser in the middle of the table to finish cleaning the rest of the drying spots of chocolate.

Poppet tipped back her head and wailed. "I just don't want to go to jail." She pointed an accusing finger at Niddie. "And you can't make me. Poppa said you had to take care of me ... of all of us. And you promised him you would. I was there! I heard you! That meant here in our house, our home. He didn't mean in jail!"

"Oh, for heaven's sake! Shut her up, will you?" Niddie snarled. The ancient table wobbled a bit as Niddie leaned on the edge before dropping back into her chair. She looked at her sobbing sister with a sigh. "You know, you really need to grow up, Poppet. You're almost 72 and you still go by your baby name, for Pete's sake. Poppa's been gone for over twenty years..."

At the mention of their father, Poppet's eyes refilled and her chin began to tremble. Niddie shook her finger at Poppet's quivering face. "Stop that blubbering! If you can't help us find a way out of this mess, then go watch your soaps."

"They aren't even on yet," Poppet sniffed and sniveled. She looked at Aggie for back up. "See! Niddie doesn't know everything!"

Aggie wisely took no sides on this issue.

Niddie felt the blood in her veins run high. She could hear a soft whooshing sound in her ears that meant she needed to calm down. She sat back against the chair and laid her hands in her lap palms up. She spent a few minutes doing the calming exercise her doctor had taught her. After a few quiet minutes of inhaling deeply and exhaling slowly, she felt the pounding in her ears settle and the pressure slowly ease. She shook her head. All she needed at this moment was to have a heart attack or stroke. She took another deep breath. As that horrible idea crossed her mind, she decided to make her youngest sister happy for the time being.

Without opening her eyes, she said to Poppet, "Then go and get a bag of Oreos and sit there quietly while Aggie and I talk."

Instantly, Poppet's eyes brightened at the idea of her favorite cookies. With a quickness belying her age, Poppet lurched out of her chair and nearly skipped across the kitchen. She hid a satisfied grin behind her hand so Niddie couldn't see the smile. Aggie always yelled at her for eating between meals, but Niddie said she could and, by jingles, she was going to enjoy this opportunity.

Aggie glared at Niddie, leaned forward on the table, and whispered loudly, "Why'd you tell her she could have cookies? You know she needs to lose weight before we go back to the doctor next month."

The old table complained loudly as Niddie leaned in and glared back. "If we don't find a way out of this mess, there isn't going to be a doctor next month ... or any other month after this one."

Both women leaned back in their chairs and listened to their sister tear into the bag that held the flimsy plastic tray filled with cookies. Several satisfied little moans later, Poppet returned to her place where she had sat since childhood.

Poppet moaned at the delicious flavor in her mouth. "Mm-m-m-m. Mm-m-m-m-m."

Sheepishly, she looked at the other two. With a few dark crumbs clinging to her chin, she shyly held out the bag of cookies to see if they wanted one. When her sisters waved her off, she smiled and cuddled the beautiful blue and white bag back to her chest and chewed happily.

Niddie looked down at her own work-worn hands. The idea of losing the land her parents had worked so hard and moving into a town apartment, no matter how close to the farm, was more than she could bear. She'd never wanted to live anywhere else and, except for her two months in the convent, Poppet never had either. Aggie was the adventurous one.

Aggie had moved away to have a family of her own and left the farm for more than 40 years. She'd traveled the world with her structural engineer husband, helped him run construction sites for multi-storied, gleaming buildings and occasionally even grabbed a pair of gloves and heaved a few shovels of dirt just for the sheer joy of working. But she'd called her sisters at least once a week and spent every holiday possible with them.

Four years ago, her husband, discontented with retirement, decided to go to Dubai on one more job. When he fell from the top story of the tower he helped design, Aggie had not hesitated to move home to be with her sisters. There was no reason not to. Her son, Jason, was in the military, moving up the ranks, and her daughter, Christine, was growing her medical career with her doctor husband. Aggie missed them terribly but, here with her sisters, she was safe and comfortable. She was home!

Aggie had to concede that Poppet was right. Their father had given Niddie the task of taking care of them and everything he'd left behind, but she'd also been asked to help. What he hadn't counted on was how much that care would cost and how little they'd have left after all this time. He also hadn't counted on that slimy little weasel, *Uncle* Bogey, he'd left in charge of the Whoodah money, who left in the night with everything. And he certainly hadn't counted old debts showing up many years later. Niddie's thoughts went back to the day before when that long black shadow had driven into their lives.

Poppet had seen the limo first. "Who is that?" She asked her sisters as she stared out the kitchen window. Aggie walked over to see the massive dark vehicle pull into the drive. As the car crept up to the front of the house, Poppet called, "Niddie! Niddie! You better get in here."

Niddie came into the kitchen and joined her sisters at the cracked window. Outside, the car stopped and a uniformed driver bounded around to open the back door. A man of about twenty-three stepped out, looking sure of himself.

"Who is that?" whispered Poppet. "He looks kinda ... slimy."

"I don't know anyone who rides in a limo around here," Aggie answered.

The cocky young man tugged at the lapels of his dark suit and looked around. His nose wrinkled as he surveyed the landscape. Clearly, this wasn't where he normally found himself.

"Obviously, a city kid," Poppet snorted derisively.

"No sense standing here wondering." Niddie turned and walked to the door. With her sisters right behind her, she stepped out onto the porch and called out, "Can I help you?"

With another sniff, the man ran his hands over the sides of his oily, slicked back hair and came toward them, stepping carefully for fear of stepping in something that would soil his highly shined shoes. "My name is Bruno Sactman." At the foot of the stairs, he reached a hand up to Niddie. "I assume you are Ms. Masterson?"

"I am," Niddie narrowed her eyes and waited for more information. She ignored the proffered hand. Sactman let his drop to his side, nonplussed by the slight.

"I have some business to talk about with you." He gestured at the chairs on the porch. "Do you mind if we sit?"

Niddie crossed her arms. "What kind of business? I don't know you!"

"Niddie!" Aggie stepped out from behind her sister. "No need to be unfriendly." She stuck her hand out to the man. "I'm Ms. Masterson's sister, Mrs. Hennenfent ... Aggie. Please come up and sit with us." She introduced Poppet. Poppet nodded and went to sit in the furthest chair. "Would you like something to drink?" Aggie asked graciously.

The man looked around at the run-down furniture and porch. He walked to the sturdiest looking chair. He sniffed again. "No," he said, "if you don't mind, I'd like to get right down to business." He pulled a kerchief out of his pocket and dusted the chair before cautiously sitting down. "I have another appointment back in town."

"How could we possibly have any business? I don't believe we've ever met," Niddie asked.

The smarmy man reached into his suit and pulled out an envelope. "You're right. We've never met, but our fathers knew each other." He handed the wrinkled old envelope to Niddie and sat back with a smug smile.

Niddie took the crumpled envelope and pulled a faded piece of paper out. The first thing she noticed was her father's signature on the bottom. As she read the document, she gasped and put a hand to her lips.

"What is that thing?" Aggie asked. Niddie handed her the page. Aggie's eyes opened wide. "An I.O.U? For $150,000?"

"I knew it!" Poppet cried out, "He's a gangster!" She threw her hands in the air and raced into the kitchen. "I bet he has a gun! In fact, I'm sure of it! Run!" Aggie tossed the letter to Niddie and followed after her terrified sister.

The man snickered. "I don't have any guns. I didn't think I'd need them with three little old ladies." He looked down at his driver who stood at the foot of the stairs, snickering as well.

"Look, I don't know what this means and I'm still not sure who you are, but do not assume we're three *defenseless* little old ladies. We're quite capable of handling our business." She looked him square in the eye and gave him her harshest librarian stare. To his credit, the man only flinched slightly.

"My father was a bookie in the city. He and your father did, uhm, business occasionally," he explained.

"Our father passed away years ago. We put an ad in the paper to call for outstanding debts before we settled his estate." Niddie snapped the page against her fingers. "This name never came up."

Sactman sat forward and stroked the sparse moustache he was trying to grow on his lip. "The kind of business our fathers did doesn't go through normal channels." He returned Niddie's stare. "My father passed away several weeks ago and I inherited his business. This note was found in a file marked "collectibles"." He sat back again. "And that's why I'm here."

"You mean you want to collect this money ... after all this time," Niddie tipped her head to one side. The man didn't move. "I suppose you want your money soon."

Again, the man didn't flinch. "Yes. Today. Oh, and I only deal in cash."

Poppet and Aggie who had returned to the doorway gasped aloud. Ignoring the two women in the doorway, Sactman paused for effect. He lifted his hand and examined his well manicured nails and, without looking up, stated, "Or you can give me the farm."

Without a moment's hesitation, Poppet grabbed the old straw broom leaning by the door and raced at the smug young man. His smile faded as she drew the broom up over her head and clouted him as hard as she could. "Get out of here! Now! You slimy worm! You mean little weasel!"

The stunned man scrambled out of the chair and tried to cover his head as he heard the swish of the straws whistling through the air near his ear. The driver stepped up, trying to help his boss and avoid being hit by the weapon Poppet swung with such accuracy.

Ducking and dodging the next well-aimed blow, Sactman screamed, "You crazy old bat! What do you think you're doing?" He waved his arms trying to protect himself while backing down the stairs toward the safety of his car.

Poppet brandished the stout, worn broom and yelled at her astonished sisters who'd never seen their portly, loveable sister give in to violence. "Go get the gun. Niddie! Aggie! Help me!"

Sactman dodged the flailing broom once more and tripped just as he reached the safety of the car. Like a skittering crab on an open beach full of seagulls, he clambered into the backseat.

"You're all crazy! You old bats!" He shook his fist at them through the tinted, barely open window.

"You have two choices! I'll give you six weeks for the money or the deed. You decide." He rolled up the window as Poppet screamed again and belted the shiny black car with her wood and straw sword.

"Get out of here, you slimy buzzard! We aren't giving you anything, you lying little snot!" Tears streaming out of her eyes, her chest heaving with anger, Poppet watched the car race down the drive, scattering dust and gravel in its wake.

Aggie came up behind her. "Well, you sure showed him, Poppet." She put her arms around her sister and turned her back to the porch. Poppet reached up and tucked an errant strand of hair behind her ear.

"Well, I just hate to act that way," Poppet sighed. "but I'm sure the good Lord will forgive me my loss of temper ... you know, considering the circumstances and all."

The three women settled into the chairs on the porch and quietly watched the cloud of dust rise up on the distant dirt road, each deep in her own thoughts.

Chapter Two

"So what can we do besides what Poppa taught us to do?" Aggie's eyes welled up as she thought about the scene in the yard on the previous evening. "Apparently, Poppa went on a gambling spree before he died. Remember when he said he was going to visit his friend in Atlantic City? Well, that must be when he ended up owing this guy $150,000. The letter's very clear and that's definitely Poppa's signature." Aggie announced, glancing at the offending letter on the table in front of her.

Poppet pushed another Oreo into her mouth and talked around the crumbs, "He looked just like one of the bad guys on TV, hair all greasy and slicked back." She began to choke a little and lifted the now chilled cup of chocolate to sip.

Niddie ran her hands over her tired face. "I know. I know." She reached across the table and snatched the nearly empty bag of cookies from her sister. "Give me those!"

Poppet gasped and started to protest. Niddie stuck a boney finger in her face.

"Don't start with the whimpering. You've had enough. Besides the crunching is annoying! If you're not going to be in this conversation, go watch television." She gestured toward the darkened living room behind her.

Poppet shuffled across the creaky floor to the door behind Niddie. Just before she went through, she turned around and stuck her Oreo-coated tongue out at Niddie's back. Aggie shook her finger at her naughty sister but Poppet smiled widely and ducked out of the room before Niddie could see her.

Niddie sat quietly for a few more seconds. She lifted her head, looked around to be sure Poppet was out of earshot, and glanced at Aggie. "We've never really had enough money to do all the things that needed doing around here. You know that, Aggie. And every year we worry about the taxes on this place. The only thing I can see is to visit Whoodah Thunket like Poppa taught us."

"But Poppa never really taught us anything. He told us about his jobs and showed us his tools. And he even let you practice on that old safe in the barn but we have never actually done a job."

"I know but I really think we can do it. We have all his tools and most of getting away with things is acting like you know what you're doing." Niddie said, not sure if she was trying to convince herself or her sister.

"And how do you think we're going to do this without Poppet's knowledge? You know she'll put up a fuss." Aggie nodded toward the suspiciously quiet living room.

"She'll either have to stay here or come and help," Niddie responded. "Her choice."

"Ok, so where would you want to go?" Aggie questioned. "You know we can't do a job around here."

"I know," snapped Niddie. "... never less than twenty miles from home. Rule number one!"

Niddie threw her hands in the air and then let them flop back onto the table with a solid thump. Aggie looked at her sister's worried face and reached out to take her hand.

"This is our last option," Niddie gave in. "We have no choice. We don't want to sell the place. That man wants his money and we already tried the bank. We just cannot add another bill to our fixed budget. Either we give him the farm or we visit Whoodah."

Aggie sank back in her chair with a heavy sigh just as another distant whooshing sound rattled the windows.

"What IS that?" Niddie asked in exasperation as she stood up and walked over to look out the window overlooking the back pastures. Nothing seemed amiss.

"I'm not sure," Aggie shook her head as if trying to remember something. "That does sound kind of familiar though."

At that moment, Poppet raced back into the kitchen. "I heard you! I heard what you said! You're not selling my house!" Sobbing, she threw herself at Aggie. "Don't let her sell out, Aggie! Don't let her!" Aggie wrapped her arms around Poppet and murmured into her bowed head.

"Relax. We're going to figure this out. Don't you worry."

Niddie returned to the table and sat down. She looked at her sisters and said, "We just need to make a plan. And, if you ..." she waggled a long bony finger at her youngest sister. "... can't help, then stay out of the way!"

Poppet pulled herself out of Aggie's arms and started to argue when Aggie stepped in front of her. She put her hands on Poppet's wide shoulders, squeezed slightly and looked deeply into the red-rimmed blue eyes.

As kindly as she could, Aggie cajoled, "Poppet, ask yourself this - who's going to buy your Oreos and pay for your cable TV if we have to pay rent to someone else on our current incomes? What will you do when we can't afford cable and cookies?"

Poppet shook her head and dropped into her chair. She'd already asked herself that question so many times. She folded her hands on the table in front of her and settled in to listen.

"Alright," Niddie sighed. "So, tomorrow, we gather up all Poppa's old tools and ..."

"Wait a minute!" Poppet narrowed her eyes at Niddie. "Poppa's tools?"

"Yes, the ones he taught us to use when he told us about Whoodah Thunket," Niddie responded.

Poppet shrieked, "I thought you said you got rid of those old things years ago?"

Niddie blushed at being caught in a lie. For all her softness, Poppet had a way of looking at you, when she caught you in a fib that made you feel very small. Niddie said softly, "No, I still have them out in the barn."

Poppet gasped and sputtered, "But we swore we'd never use them! Why did you save them?"

Her eyes narrowed again. She pointed an accusatory finger at Niddie's nose. "You never meant to keep your oath, did you?"

"I'm not going to argue about this. I need some air. I'm going for a ride if I can catch the danged horse." Niddie stood. "If you can come up with a better idea, I'm all for doing something else."

As she strode out of the room, Poppet whispered to Aggie. "Do you think she's lost her mind? Did she forget what going to visit Whoodah Thunket means?" Poppet's eyes got round and big. "Maybe she's got that old timer's disease!!"

"No, her mind's fine," Aggie assured her. "We all remember quite well what Whoodah means."

Poppet let her voice raise into a louder whisper. "You mean she really wants us to become ... criminals!? For real?" Poppet continued indignantly, "Then I hope that horse makes her chase him for an hour before she gets to ride him!" She crossed her arms and harrumphed under her breath.

Aggie looked down at her cold tea. The two women sat in uneasy silence. Poppet wondered if her soaps had started yet while Aggie thought back to the night they were finally told about Whoodah and what that name really meant.

Chapter Three

As soon as they were old enough to figure things out, Niddie and Aggie had one of their frequent late night secret chats. Niddie was the one who suggested that when their father had gone out late at night saying he had to go visit the mysterious Whoodah Thunket, he was cheating on their mother. Aggie didn't want to believe the possibility. But all the evidence pointed to Whoodah being some slinky dame on the other side of the town. Niddie's best friend had filled her in on slinky dames and all that stuff when she was thirteen. Niddie's friend knew all about them since her dad had run off with one the year before.

When they confronted him with their certain knowledge, Poppa burst out laughing and pulled them into a smothering hug. After telling them how much he loved them and their mother, he took the girls to the old shed in the back where they were never allowed to go. There he told them that Whoodah Thunket was just his little code name for his part time *job*. They were completely floored.

"What do you mean you rob houses?" 17-year-old Niddie bellowed indignantly. "You mean you climb in windows and steal things?"

Her father shushed her. "Now listen. I lost my job a long time ago and I didn't have the heart to tell you or your momma about what I'm doing. I've been doing these little jobs with Uncle Bogey for a long time now.

Aggie shook her head. "But we rent out the fields and sell the hay. Why do you need to be a thief?"

Poppa took her hands in his. "All those things don't make enough money to keep three young ladies in school. Niddie wants to go to college. I'm sure you and Poppet have plans too. When your momma got sick, I had to make more money and I sure didn't want her to worry about anything. So Uncle Bogey and I started this little business."

"Little business!" Aggie cried. "You've been breaking the law! If you get caught, you'll go to jail. Then what will we do?"

Niddie tipped her head to one side and narrowed her eyes. "So all those times you kissed momma ... and us ... and walked out the door saying you were going to visit Whoodah, you weren't going to see another woman?"

"Good lord no! I've always loved your mother."

"And momma knew all about what you're doing?" Aggie questioned.

"Well, she knows as much as she ever wanted to know."

"And you've never gotten caught?" Aggie continued.

"Nope!" Poppa explained. "First, we have rules and they protect us from getting caught. Second, Uncle Bogey takes care of all the details and the money for us. Most importantly, we only go when we have to and we never, ever pull a job close by here."

"*Uncle* Bogey!?" Niddie scoffed. "That slimy little man is not my uncle! Momma told me that *bogarting* means you keep everything for yourself. That's how he got his nickname because he bogarts everything! He's so greedy he doesn't like to share anything. And you really trust him ... with your money? With your safety?"

Poppa sat upright, put his hands out toward them and made a pushing motion. "Calm down, Niddie. I know your momma never trusted him either, but Bogey has never crossed me."

"Ha! That you know of," Aggie scoffed. "Why does he get to keep the money?"

"Everyone knows Bogey gambles," Poppa explained. "That's why the best plan is to let him keep the money. Whenever he's gone for a day or two and comes back with extra money, everyone just assumes he hit a lucky streak. He always has lots of money. If I had a lot of money all of a sudden, people would get suspicious."

"But Poppa," Aggie said, "you gamble too."

Poppa smiled shyly and touched her cheek. "Yes, but I'm not as good as Bogey. And I don't gamble as big or as often as Bogey does ... since I have my family to worry about. Bogey gambles big and wins a lot more than he loses."

Poppa continued, "Anyway, we have enough money to take care of everything now for a long time. No one will be going to visit Whoodah Thunket ... hopefully, ever again." He pulled both girls in another tight hug. "So just calm down and forget about this. Oh, and let's not tell Poppet. You know how easily she gets upset."

And forget they did. Life got in the way. A few weeks later, momma passed away and, in his sorrow, poppa began drinking much more. Niddie started college. Aggie met her future husband and moved away. Poppet carried on in blissful ignorance as always.

Then came the day three years later, Poppa called Aggie and Niddie to the kitchen table and said, "Girls, we have to talk. I need your help." Poppet overheard them and all hell broke loose.

A week later, Poppet ran away to the convent.

Chapter Four

"Yoo hoo! I'm back!" Aggie called excitedly, coming through the front door, stopping to drop her coat and purse on the wooden bench in the foyer. "Where is everyone? I think I have our target."

Poppet stopped scrubbing the lunch dishes and Niddie poked her head around the corner of the upstairs hallway. Aggie waved at her sisters. "Come into the library and I'll tell you all about what I learned! And bring some tea! I could really use a good cuppa."

The women gathered in the room that once was their mother's sewing room and the family library. When Momma passed away, the sewing machine, bolts of cloth and spools of threads had disappeared into boxes to be replaced by their books. All three women were voracious readers. The surrounding shelves almost groaned with the weight of all the read, as-yet-unread and might-never-be-read books they had gathered over the years. In the middle of the room stood a large table rescued from a pile of discarded church furniture. The scarred wood on the table were laden with more books, newspapers, and other materials that might be needed.

Aggie slid into her favorite comfy chair and waited. Seconds later, Niddie came around the corner carrying a tray of cups and saucers. Behind her came Poppet, a bag of Oreos under one arm and a pot of tea carefully held between her hands. Poppet set the teapot down and went to the chair Momma had always sat in. She tried to quietly slip the bag of cookies between her and the arm of the chair but the crinkly sound brought a scowl from Niddie as she dropped into Poppa's old high-backed chair.

"Poppet!"

Poppet didn't even look at Niddie who began pouring the tea. Poppet didn't need to see the disapproving glare to know she'd been caught. Darn that crinkling, loud wrapper! She slid the bag lovingly on to the table top, careful to keep the treasure within her reach.

A few minutes later with tea poured and feet up on the worn foot stool Poppa had used for so many years, Niddie encouraged her sister. "So tell us."

Aggie took a sip of the hot tea, letting the liquid slip through her and warm every aching bone in her body. *The Brits really knew what they were talking about when they said that a spot of tea could fix anything,* she thought.

"Well, I was in town this morning, mailing those things over to the Doctors Without Boarders camp in Africa for Christine and Randolph."

Poppet perked up. "Oh! I can't wait till they come home and see what they bring me! I just love having a niece who travels to such exciting places. How long till they come home?"

Aggie smiled, but waved Poppet off. "I'll have to check later. But let me tell you what happened this morning. I went by Mary Jane's Coffee Shop down on Frost Street. I was just going to have a cup of coffee before coming home."

"Coffee?" Niddie clucked her tongue and shook her head. "You know that messes with your stomach."

"I know, but I just felt like one little cup that early in the morning would be ok ... anyway, who should be in there, but Margie Robbins. You remember her. She was in middle school with us and then was held back a year. We sort of lost touch when she stayed back." Both sisters muttered and nodded that they remembered. "Well, she told me that her family had moved in her sophomore year. She finished school, got married and had kids. But last year, her husband had died without leaving her very well off and she felt like coming back here." Aggie paused for effect and took another sip of her tea.

"Why is this important to our problem?" Niddie asked peevishly.

"I'm getting to that," Aggie explained softly. "All those years she worked as a maid in big fancy houses in the city. So, when she came here, she found a job with the Bradenton family over in Tractown!"

Poppet's eyes grew wide. "In that big old house out in the middle of nowhere? That's gotta be at least thirty miles away."

Niddie sighed. "Poppa always thought that place would make a good mark, but he had no way of figuring out what's in there."

"But now," Aggie smiled slyly and then winked at her sisters. "I think Whoodah Thunket would approve of this target."

Niddie raised her brows and started to take a sip from her cup. "Do tell," she encouraged over the lip of the thin china.

Poppet stood up and paced the small room wringing her hands, shaking her head and murmuring nope, no way, no, over and over. "Ohhhhh, I can't go there!"

Niddie looked at Aggie and rolled her eyes. "What's the problem now?" Niddie asked, exasperation dripping from her voice.

"Don't you remember that big stairway in the foyer?" The two older women looked puzzled.

Poppet returned to her chair. "You HAVE to remember. We went there for Buddy Bradenton's 12th birthday party. That was one of the worst days of my life."

Aggie sighed. "I remember the party, but I sure don't remember anything traumatic."

Poppet jumped up again. "That's because you weren't there!" She cried out.

"I don't remember anything either, Poppet. You're being foolish!"

Poppet burst into tears. "Buddy tried to kill me on those stairs. I've had vertigo on stairways every since."

Niddie's cup and saucer clattered loudly as she set them down on the table. "I've never heard of this vertigo thing before."

"Well, it's true," sobbed Poppet between her fingers.

Aggie stood and went to her little sister's side. She guided Poppet back to her chair and sat down on the arm. "Tell me what happened."

"I was coming back from the bathroom. Just as I got to the top of the stairs, Buddy ran past me and I lost my balance. I fell forward and grabbed the handrail to save myself but I still fell off the top stair. I hung there almost upside down trying to get my footing for a few minutes with Buddy and his friends laughed and made fun of me. I had to save myself while those mean boys laughed."

Niddie sniffed. "So now all of a sudden you're afraid of staircases?"

"No," Poppet sneered, "just tall steep ones. Mostly just that one."

Niddie pinched the bridge of her nose for a moment. When she took her hand down, she turned to Aggie without another word to Poppet.

"Go on!" Niddie pressed her sister. "Go on!"

Aggie returned to her place, picked up her cup from the little wooden side table next to her chair, leaned forward and asked, "What do you remember most about Margie?"

"I know! I know!" Poppet practically bounced in her chair. "She had a great big mouth! Never stopped talking and couldn't keep a secret to save her life!! Everyone called her Motor-mouth Margie!"

"Right! And she hasn't changed a bit!" Aggie exclaimed. Poppet clapped her hands together like a gleeful tot who got the right answer in school. She reached for the bag of Oreos to celebrate, but Niddie got there first. The bag was snatched out of Poppet's reach before her hand crossed the table's edge. Poppet wrinkled her nose and sat back with a loud hrumpf.

"So, after talking to her for half an hour, I found out she's angry because she has to take an unpaid week off starting next week because the Bradentons are going on a two-week cruise. The house will be all locked up, but get this. The top floor isn't wired. Poor Margie just didn't understand that because the safe is up there in the master bedroom and Mrs. Bradenton always forgets to close the safe up!"

This time even Niddie gasped in delight.

"Oh, and I found out another thing." Aggie picked up her cup, drained her tea, set the cup back on the table and stood. She elaborately brushed invisible crumbs off her lap and then looked at her expectant sisters. "Poppet was right."

Poppet, who loved being right, jumped up clapping her hands. "Yes! I knew it! I knew I was right!" She looked at Niddie who always knew everything and wrinkled her nose. Niddie looked back, eyebrows lifted as if in question. Poppet dropped her hands to her sides and turned back to Aggie. "Right about what?"

Aggie walked toward the door. "I'm hungry. Is lunch ready?"

"Aggie!" shouted Poppet. "Right about what?"

"Oh, uhm, right," she looked at Niddie. "There's a company looking around for mineral deposits. They're in the next county, moving this way. I knew that whoosh sound was familiar. Apparently, they set off small dynamite charges sometimes!"

Aggie continued to the kitchen, followed by the excited Poppet, while Niddie stayed in the big chair and mused over the announcement.

Chapter Five

"Are you sure?" Poppet whispered. "Absolutely certain?"

The three women stood in the shadows and stared at the expanse of manicured lawn that separated them and the house. At their feet lay a 16-foot wooden ladder that had definitely seen many workmen's boots. Standing there so long in the damp night under the trees surrounding the huge house had Niddie chilled to the bone. She knew her sisters were feeling the cold as well. They needed to get up and move around before they stiffened up too much to move.

"Let's get going then," Aggie whispered. "What are we waiting for?"

Niddie snickered, feeling a bit silly. "I guess I'm just a little nervous."

"True, but we've done our homework. Just like Poppa told us ..." They heard a sniffle behind them. Both whipped their heads around and threatened Poppet with a "don't you start again" glare. Poppet snuffed back the tears.

"I just don't know why I have to be here. Can't I just sit in the car and watch for intruders?"

"Poppet, you forget ..." Niddie scoffed. "We're the intruders! Besides you have that vertigo thing to worry about."

Poppet shrugged. "You know what I mean. I could just go back to the car and whistle if I see anyone coming."

Niddie shook her head in disbelief. "First, I have never heard you whistle once in your life. Second, the car is more than a quarter mile away. Third, we need you to help with the ladder. That thing's way too heavy for the two of us to carry alone. So just suck it up and be quiet."

Poppet whimpered, "So I have to stay outside? By myself? In the dark and cold?"

Aggie groaned. "Yes, Poppet, that's the plan. You steady the ladder while we go in and when we come out."

"But I don't want to be alone in the dark outside." The whiney voice rose an octave.

"Shhhhh. Knock off the bickering you two," snapped Niddie. She tugged the black wool cap down further over her ears trying to block out the sniveling. "Poppet, you made your decision. You said you're afraid to climb up the ladder to the second story. You chose to stay down here. And, besides," Niddie paused and wiped a hand over her face. "Poppet, I don't mean this to be mean but, honestly, I don't think you can get in quietly."

Poppet sat straight up and pulled herself up to her full height. "What are you saying ...?"

"I'm saying that you might not be able to climb that high ... with your vertigo and all."

Poppet sniffed and sagged back down to her normal posture. "Well, maybe ..."

"Let's get this over with, girls. Put your gloves on," Aggie pulled on Niddie's arm. The women tugged gloves onto their fingers, reached down and grabbed their assigned rung of the ladder - Niddie at the front, Aggie in the rear and the still sniffling Poppet supporting the middle. Poppet muttered as they walked around the manicured lawn, staying in the shadows, "I could climb. I'm the youngest. I could probably scamper right up that ladder. You know ... if not for the vertigo and all."

"Scamper!" Aggie laughed with a scoff. "None of us can scamper any more." Aggie looked up at the rambling house.

Here on the eastern side, a slightly open window waited for them. Fortunately, the second floor was shielded from the driveway. The window had nothing but bare wall below it. With one end of the ladder over her right shoulder and her sisters in step behind her, Niddie walked toward the window until she was close enough to lift the ladder up against the wall. She lifted her end of the cumbersome wooden structure up as high as she could and held the long beams as steady. When the ladder finally leaned against the bottom of the window, Aggie stood back and dusted her hands. "Whew! That's not as easy as it used to be."

Sarcasm dripped as Niddie snapped. "So what is?" She put a foot on the bottom rung of the ladder. "Aggie, as soon as I'm in, you bring the other stuff. And you..." she pointed at Poppet who needed to be kept busy. "... you stay here and warn us in case anyone comes by."

With that, she clambered up the ladder to the window. Her father's tools hung in a neat array from her waist and jangled slightly with each step. Niddie wasn't really worried about anyone coming by the house. *This little town hadn't had a robbery in* ... Niddie tried to remember how long. *The police probably didn't even remember how to read a crime scene any more,* she thought with a snarky smile on her face.

She shook her head to refocus her thoughts as she slipped her gloved fingers under the bottom of the window and pressed up. Carefully, trying not to lean backwards, she lifted the window to full open. As soon as she was successful, she waved down at her sisters and crawled out of view.

Once inside, Niddie crouched on the floor, knees and back aching from the climb. She took a few precious seconds to steady her breath. Between climbing the ladder and the adrenaline rush, her heart was pounding much too fast. When her eyes grew accustomed to the darkness in the room, she stood up and started to step away from the window when she thought she heard Aggie call out a soft warning. The ladder scraped against the wall as the wood bent under the weight of someone climbing.

"I'm not staying out here alone." Poppet's whiney voice came through the open window.

"Oh, for the love of ..." Niddie returned to the window and looked down. There was Poppet halfway up the ladder. Aggie was only a few rungs below her. "What are you doing?"

"I'm scared, Niddie. I don't want to stay out in the dark alone."

Exasperated, Niddie rubbed a gloved hand over her face and called softly down. "Fine. Get in here." She leaned out the window to offer a hand. At that moment, Poppet looked down. When she realized how far off the ground she was, she gasped and wrapped her arms tightly around the ladder.

"I-I-I c-c-can't m-m-m-ove, Niddie! I'll fall!" Poppet's wail cut through the quiet night. "I'm getting my vertigo, just like in the movie!"

Niddie cursed mightily under her breath, leaned out as far as she could and commanded, "Give me your hand."

"No! If I let go, I'll fall!"

"Prudence Margaret, you give me your hand right now! Close your eyes and reach up. You know I won't let you fall."

Slowly, the whimpering Poppet did as she was told. She loosened her clenched fingers and slid the palm of her gloved hand along the rough wood. As her arm reached the end of its stretch, she felt Niddie's strong fingers wrap around her hand. She grabbed tightly.

"Don't pull, you fool!" Niddie gasped and then tugged at Poppet's hand. "Take one step up."

"NO!! I can't."

"Oh, for crying in a bucket! Aggie, where are you?"

The muffled sound of Aggie's voice whispered, "I'm right behind her. Just a couple rungs down."

"Well, put a shoulder into her and push!" Niddie demanded. Aggie climbed high enough to wedge her shoulder under her sister's ample backside. Poppet cried out as her plump body began to move upward whether she wanted to climb or not. Niddie pulled and Aggie pushed. They worked their way upward – step by rickety step. When Poppet felt the edge of the window scrape her arm, she let go of Niddie's hand, grabbed the sill and pulled herself up a bit more. "Let me go. I can do this now."

Niddie sniffed and let herself fall back on the plush carpet. She heard Aggie whisper, "Then move! I don't have much more strength left here."

Poppet climbed another rung until she could flop half her body onto the window ledge. Instantly, she knew she'd misjudged how far she was inside. "Uhm ... Niddie?" She knew Niddie was nearby but couldn't see her.

"What!?"

"Uhm, I'm kinda ... uhm, stuck!"

"What do you mean - kinda?"

"Well, I'm half in. My feet are off the ladder. I just can't tip inside."

"I swear, Poppet, when we get home ..."

Aggie's gasping voice whispered, "Threaten her later, will you!? I'm losing my grip here." Niddie rose back up and grabbed Poppet's wide shoulders.

"Push, Aggie, push!"

Poppet could feel her body press further into the window ledge. Aggie lifted Poppet's support hose covered legs onto her shoulders. Poppet felt a cool breeze ruffle the skirt she now regretted she had insisted on wearing. Her arms were being pulled out of their sockets and the wood was cutting into her belly. She yelled, "Owww, you're hurting me, Niddie!"

"Shut up, Poppet! Aggie!" Niddie called. "Can you push her up any more?"

Aggie called back breathlessly. "I'll try. She's just far enough in that she's balancing like a teeter totter! Every time you pull her, her legs fly into the air and I lose touch!"

As she said that, Niddie pulled once again. Poppet squealed as her legs flew up and her arms were stretched. Aggie stepped up one rung and grabbed Poppet's legs. "Try rocking her side to side!"

"Noooooo!" Poppet cried out as she felt herself tipped to the left and then quickly to the right. "I'm gonna be sick!"

"Hush," Niddie groaned and sat back on her heels.

"Do that once more," Aggie called from below. "She's almost in!"

An exasperated blast of air flew from Niddie's lips as she took hold of Poppet's arms for one more try. "Poppet," she muttered, "if this doesn't work, I'm going to push you back out."

"But ..."

"No buts," Niddie snarled as she braced her feet against the wall under the window and pulled once more. "If you don't want to fall and take Aggie with you, you better get through this window."

Thinking of falling and hurting her sister gave Poppet the extra impetus she needed. "Pull me Niddie! Push me Aggie!" Poppet began to rock herself side to side.

"She's moving," Aggie triumphantly cried out.

Teeth grinding, Niddie snarled, "You should have. Stayed. Outside." With each groaned word, Niddie gave a strong tug. Poppet's plump body inched in the window. One final pull, a squeal of pain and Poppet fell through the window into

Niddie's lap. Niddie struggled to get her breath back and wondered if this was worth the battle. Aggie climbed in behind Poppet.

Poppet started to giggle. Both Niddie and Aggie looked at her in surprise. Poppet put a hand to her mouth and the other up palm out toward her sisters, snickering wildly. In a few seconds, she dropped her hands away from her face and said, "For a few minutes there, I was a great "poppet" totter." She laughed. "Get it? Poppet totter instead of teeter totter?"

Aggie smiled and patted Poppet's hand. Niddie turned away.

"You people have no sense of humor sometimes," Poppet whispered. Niddie whipped around again.

"Yeah, yippee. Fun. We don't have time for fun." Niddie sniggered. "Darn good thing no one is home. Let's get going."

Anxious to prove she could be of help, Poppet called, "I'll get the ladder." She leaned over the edge and lifted the legs leaning against the house just as both sisters cried out, "No!" Poppet jumped at the loud cries and the ladder slipped from her hands. The sisters held their breath and listened to the ladder fall away from the house with a loud clattering scraping crash. Sheepishly, Poppet turned to face her sisters. Two sets of eyes glared at her. She raised her hands in protest.

"What?" she whined, "I mean, surely you weren't planning to go back down that way."

"That was the plan, Poppet!" Niddie glared at her, hands on hips, anger dripping off her entire body.

"Well, that was a terrible idea," Poppet dusted her arms off, ignoring her sister's obvious fury. With a sniff, she turned away to look at Aggie.

"I know," Aggie moaned. "But we don't need the extra noise either."

"But nobody can hear us." Poppet whined.

"Shut up you two!" Niddie demanded. "Let's get what we came for." She grabbed Poppet's shoulder and aimed her for the door. "Aggie, you go to the master bedroom. You remember where the suite is?"

"Of course, about three doors down on the left."

"Good." Niddie grabbed Poppet's arm. "And you stay behind me. And be quiet. You've caused enough trouble for the night."

They opened the door and began to walk toward the master suite. Tiptoeing down the thickly carpeted hall, the women found the bedroom and entered. The mirror that disguised the safe was hanging on the far wall just as the maid had described. Poppet tiptoed across the room, tucked her fingers under the side of the mirror and tried to tug the mirror. "This is heavy and stuck on the wall."

"Wait," Aggie said, walking quickly across the room, and stood looking at the mirror. "Margie said there was a latch on the bottom."

Niddie joined her sisters. Reaching down to the bottom of the ornate mirror, she ran her nimble fingers along the edge until she felt a small clasp. As she slipped the piece of metal aside, the mirror swung open. There was the safe, and just as the maid had told her, the door was slightly ajar.

Poppet stepped back, clasped her hands to her cheeks, and cried, "Okay, I can't do this part. This is the really bad part that a proper nun would never do."

Niddie growled, "Like a proper nun would break into a house instead of waiting outside."

"No time for that now, Niddie," Aggie rolled her eyes and sighed, "Get over to the door then, Poppet, and watch the hall. Niddie, hurry up! I want to get out of here! And don't take more then we need."

"I know!" Niddie snarled as she sifted through the plump envelopes in the safe. Most of them were just papers until the last one. She looked in and saw a thick stack of paper money. She was just pushing the mirror back in to place when she heard Aggie draw in a sharp breath.

"Freeze!" Aggie warned. "Was that a car door?"

Poppet started to say something, but Aggie hushed her immediately. Niddie looked at her sisters where they stood frozen in their tracks. Lifting a shushing finger to her lips, Niddie slipped over and looked through the slightly open door down the hall.

From the first floor, they heard a key turn and a door creak, followed by a tuneless whistle. Footsteps shuffled across the wooden floor of the huge foyer. A heavy thud and the tinkle of keys hitting wood echoed through the house. The steps stopped and a muttered curse broke into the whistle. The sound of the keys being placed on a table cued the whistle to start again. The women stood stiff, holding their collective breath.

The phone rang from the bedside table behind them. Aggie whipped around and slapped a hand against Poppet's mouth as she prepared to cry out. Wide-eyed, Poppet looked from one to another over Aggie's hand as both sisters whispered viciously, "Shut up!" A male voice talking to someone on the phone drifted up the stairs toward where they stood. Niddie closed the door again.

"That can only be Buddy Bradenton," Niddie looked at Poppet's brimming eyes. "Can you keep quiet?"

Poppet nodded. Niddie checked with Aggie and she slowly removed her hand.

"Whatawegonnado? Whatawegonnado?" Poppet stood wringing her hands, softly murmuring the mantra again and again.

Niddie, who was trying to think, threatened, "If you can't keep quiet, I will fix that. I brought duct tape." Silence fell heavily. Poppet's eyes flew open at the idea of what Niddie might do with the tape. The clock beside the bed behind them ticked loudly.

"OK, here's what we do. Since we can't go out the way we came in ..." Niddie glared meaningfully at Poppet who shrunk closer to Aggie. "... we'll have to go down the stairs." Poppet wanted to say she hadn't meant to push the ladder away from the window and the loss of their very dangerous way out wasn't her fault, but Niddie's glare stopped her words.

The gray curls that poked out from under the black stocking cap on Poppet's head shook violently. As she began to voice her disagreement,

Aggie lifted a hand. In the soft light, Poppet saw the huge ring of duct tape dangling from one finger. "I'll help her." Shocked at her middle sister's betrayal, Poppet placed her own hand over her mouth and backed up against the wall.

Aggie turned to Niddie. "OK, I figure he'll come up those stairs, come in here, strip off and then go to the bathroom." Poppet clamped her own hands tighter over her mouth at the words 'strip off'. Niddie nodded in agreement. "All we have to do is hide somewhere till he goes into the bathroom and then sneak out."

"What if he doesn't close the bathroom door?" Poppet whispered.

"He's wealthy," Niddie snapped. "Most wealthy people have enough manners to close the door when they're in the bathroom."

Poppet raised her hand like a timid first grader in need. Niddie ignored her sister. Poppet reached out and tapped Niddie's shoulder.

"What now?" When she turned, Poppet pointed to the wall.

In a stage whisper, she formed words slowly and carefully. "Whaaaat aboooout the saaaaaffffe?"

"I closed the mirror most of the way. I doubt he'll notice anything." The oldest sister hissed.

"Shh-h-h-h-h!" The voice downstairs had stopped. Once again, the shoes tapped against the hardwood floor. Light switches clicked in their wake. The first stair groaned loudly as the humming man climbed to the second floor. The sisters scrambled into a huddle in the middle of the room. Hearts pounding, blood roaring in their ears, fear racing up their arms and legs, they clung together for a moment. Then, as usual, Niddie took charge. "In there." She pointed to the small closet door across from the bed.

Aggie argued, "We can't get in there - not all three of us. That thing is jammed full. I looked."

Niddie pointed to the bed. "You wanna see what's under there instead?"

The gaggle of sisters waddled over to the closet. Aggie reached out and pulled the smallish door open. As she said, the little room was full, top to bottom, floor to ceiling. She pushed against a couple boxes which shifted creating a bit more space. She turned around and backed in gingerly until she felt a box press into her calves. Carefully, she pressed herself in as far as she could. She reached out, grabbed Poppet by the waist and spun her around. Poppet let her body be hauled backwards inside the cramped space. Just before she was in, she gasped, "I can't ... Aggie, wait! My foot's turned.

With the sound of the steps coming closer, there was no time to wait. Poppet grunted as Niddie shoved her bulk in, trapping both the sisters against the boxes stacked under the hanging clothes, pushed her way inside and struggled to pull the door closed. Aggie fell onto the boxes behind her and Poppet plopped heavily into her lap. Niddie's weight was added a second later. Soft moans rose from the bottom of the pile.

"Don't move!" Niddie snapped softly.

"I can't breathe," Aggie struggled to get enough air into her lungs and strength in her arms to push her sister to the side just a little. As soon as she could speak, she growled, "I've had enough of this, Poppet. Money or not, no more Oreos for you!" Poppet whimpered quietly.

"Poppet. You're squashing me! I can't ..."

There was a short silence. "Oh, oh! Sorry." Poppet said sheepishly.

Niddie was about to ask what the problem was when a distinct odor hit her nose. "Poppet!"

"I'm sorry but you're squishing my tummy. I can't help normal body functions. Remember the burritos we had for dinner last night?"

"No more Oreos and no more burritos either!" Addie gagged from beneath the pile. "From now on only bread and water." Niddie stopped Poppet's cry with a hand over her mouth.

All three stiffened as they heard the man enter the bedroom and move around. The sound of a jacket hitting the floor and a small grunt as he removed his shoes told them what he was doing. The shoes clattered softly to the carpeted floor. A jingle announced the removal of his belt. There was near silence as they envisioned him removing his shirt and then heard the pants hit the floor.

From the depths of the closet, Aggie prayed fervently that he wouldn't need anything from in here but would - quickly - go into the bathroom. Then she stifled a nervous giggle as she pictured the look on his face if he did open the door to their little dungeon. She pulled her left arm out from between her and Poppet and clasped her hand over her own mouth as she struggled not to laugh out loud.

The footsteps, muffled by the deep carpet, moved away. As soon as they heard the bathroom door close and water start running, Niddie whipped the closet door open and edged out. Poppet pulled Aggie up behind her. Aggie rubbed her ribs and eyed Poppet angrily. She put her lips to Poppet's ear and whispered, "When we get home, you're going to go on a hunger strike like all good nuns and do one of them fasting things."

Poppet gasped! Niddie grabbed her by the arm and spun her around. "We don't have time for this now. Let's get out of here."

The women slipped out the bedroom door one by one, walking as quickly and quietly as they could to the top of the steep curving stairs. Niddie and Aggie stepped down the stairs one careful step at a time.

When she reached the bottom, Niddie turned to see Poppet still at the top. Niddie glared up at her, nodded angrily and pointed to the floor beside her. Poppet shook her head hard and reached out her hand as if asking Niddie to come and get her. Niddie pursed her lips and mouthed, "Don't make me come up and get you."

"What if I make the steps squeak?" whispered Poppet. "What if I fall?"

At that moment, they heard the creak of the faucet shutting off. Poppet shot off the landing and quietly raced down to her sisters. The women ran as quietly as possible for the front door as fast as their orthopedic shoes could carry them. As they were going through the door, they heard a voice at the top of the stairs call, "Alice? Is that you, darling? Come on up. I'm waiting for you, Baby."

Teenage girl hysteria swarmed around the trio as they slipped out the front door and into the cover of the bushes next to the driveway, "OK. Let's get out of here." Niddie ordered, stifling her giggles.

"Wait." Aggie countermanded. She stepped into the light at the corner of the house. In her gloved hand, she held a fat brown leather wallet. She opened the side slit and pulled out a large wad of bills. She looked at her sisters who stood with mouths gaping open. "What? I grabbed the wallet off the table as we went by! This is pay back for laughing at our Poppet!" She tossed the wallet over her shoulder onto the porch and tucked her arm under Poppet's arm. "He'll find the thing in the morning," she snickered. "Or maybe Alice will."

Chapter Six

"Pack enough for two weeks!" Aggie yelled down the hall toward Poppet's room.

"Niddie said our trip wouldn't take that long," argued Poppet.

"Two weeks! At least!" Aggie responded.

Poppet darted around the corner into Aggie's room. "I don't know how I can stay away for two whole weeks. I have obligations to church and my other volunteer jobs. And besides who will feed the animals for that long?"

Aggie folded another shirt and pressed the clothing into the scarred old suitcase. "I've already talked to the Johnson twins. I think they can handle feeding the horse, two cats, a dog and a few hens." She closed the lid of the suitcase and leaned on the top. "Father Emerson has already agreed to find someone else to call bingo. And I'm sure someone else can put away those few books in the church library!"

Poppet huffed. "Fine, but I still think I should stay here."

"We need you for look out. You know that." Aggie latched the locks on the suitcase and picked the battered case up. She walked to the door and set the bag near Poppet's feet. Arms akimbo, she looked at Poppet's downcast face. "Listen, sweetie. I don't want to do this anymore than you do, but no one can figure another way to get the money. The first job only got us about a third of what we need."

Poppet looked up, her face morose. "I know, but doing this is just wrong. Besides," Poppet's eyes welled up. "I didn't do such a great job last time. Maybe Niddie won't want me to come."

Aggie walked over to her and gently squeezed Poppet's shoulders. "Think of this as a second chance to show Niddie you can do this! Go finish packing. We have to leave in an hour."

Poppet brightened and started out the door to return to her packing.

At that moment, the windows and doors rattled. WHOOOOOSH! The sound of a distant explosion scared the two women into each other's arms. Poppet gasped. Aggie stood holding Poppet steady and waited for something to fall off a shelf somewhere. They heard the back door slam as Niddie came in, yelling.

"Dang those men! They're scaring the hell out of the chickens. We don't have a single egg and I can't get Choteau to settle enough to get a bit in his mouth."

She groused all the way up the stairs. When she rounded the corner and saw her sisters trembling in each other's arms, she threw down her coat. "I have had enough of this madness! I'm going to town and tell them what I think of their operation. I'm telling you I've had enough!"

"Don't get upset, Niddie. The explosions are just unexpected - that's all! No real damage so far." Aggie shook herself loose from Poppet and reached out to grab Niddie's arm. "No one's hurt. Leave this upset for now, Niddie. We have to get on that plane. We'll sort this problem out when we get home."

"Tell that to the chickens," Niddie muttered as she shook off Aggie's hand and went to her own room to finish packing. Aggie and Poppet heard her cussing and muttering under her breath the whole time. Both knew better than to talk to an angry Niddie.

A loud banging on the front door commanded their attention. The two sisters stepped into the hallway.

"Who in Heaven's name could that be?" Aggie sighed.

Niddie came around the corner from her room looking at her watch. "Well, the taxi's not due for another forty minutes." She shrugged and walked toward the stairwell. "You two keep packing. I'll get rid of whoever it is."

Niddie stomped down the stairs, still muttering under her breath. Arriving at the door, she paused for a second to stiffen her backbone and furrowed her brow into her angriest glare. Then, with authority, she jerked the handle forcefully, intending to roar at the person on the other side. Instantly, she was taken aback.

The silver-haired man who stood on the other side smiling at her actually took her breath away. Never in her life had she felt such a strong presence. Not only was he tanned and, though dusty, well dressed, he was one of the few people Niddie had ever met whom she had to actually look up at in order to see his face.

The low baritone voice slipped through the screen door like a warm ice cream scoop through vanilla swirl. "I'm so sorry to bother you, ma'am, but I'd like to speak with you for a few minutes." He tugged at the brim of his Stetson and smiled more broadly. "I promise what I have to say won't take up much time."

Niddie mentally shook herself and reminded herself that she was angry at everyone ... no matter how strikingly handsome the face was or how intense those deep blue eyes might be.

"No!" She said firmly and stepped back to push the door shut. At the same moment, the man pulled the screen door open and actually placed the toe of his boot in to block the door from closing. Though he didn't step inside, Niddie stared at the toe in astonishment for a long second, fighting the urge to step back. She straightened to her full height and glared at the man with her strongest librarian glare. The man seemed unfazed. He leaned in slightly and gently asked.

"Please? This is really important, Ms. Masterson."

Niddie's brow knit at his use of her name. She was absolutely certain she didn't know this man.

Seeing her reaction, the man broadened his smile to show dazzling white teeth.

Oh, my God, thought Niddie as she felt her shoulders sag slightly. *It's the Marlboro man!*

Once again, she firmed her stance. "I'm afraid we're on our way out the door and on a tight deadline. There's no time now."

"I understand you're going to visit your niece. That's why I need to meet with you today. You see, I'm also on a pressing deadline."

"Dang town gossips!" Niddie scoffed. "No one in that place can keep their mouths shut. Telling a perfect stranger we're going out of town." Niddie put her loose hand on her hip and gripped the door knob tighter with the other. "For all they know, you're a burglar out here to case the joint. Who are you anyway?"

The handsome man reached up and took off his hat. He bowed slightly. "Most of the people in town know me by now. I've been here for a couple months and spoken with many of them. I'm Frank Moore. I'm the chief engineer for the oil ..."

"You!" Niddie all but screamed at him. Her eyes narrowed as she stepped menacingly toward him. This time he did back up a step. Reaching up to poke him in the chest, she growled. "My chickens won't lay! My horse is too skittish to ride! My cows are going dry and my poor sister has the shakes so bad she can barely sleep."

"That's not true!" From behind her came Poppet's voice. Niddie whipped around and narrowed her eyes at her sister. Both women stood on the stairway staring at the stranger who seemed to fill the porch. She pointed up the stairs and yelled, "Get back up there and finish packing!" Both women, despite their ages, clambered back up the stairs to do as they were commanded.

Niddie whipped back around in time to see the obnoxious man try to hide his grin. "Get out! I have no time or desire to speak to you." Her knees felt slightly weak, but Niddie wasn't sure if her anger or his dazzling smile made them feel that way. She pressed her hand to her chest and felt her thumping heart.

"At least take this." He reached out and took her hand. His fingers completely surrounded Niddie's. The warmth of his skin traveled up Niddie's arm, through her body and seemed to bolt her to the floor. He pressed a business card into her hand. "Maybe you can call me when you get back. I think I may have some very good news for you."

Niddie made herself pull away. She backed through the opening and, just before slamming the wooden door shut, yelled, "I completely doubt that!" The door met the jamb with a resounding thud. Niddie stumbled back until she felt the end post of the stairway press into her back. Through the curtain, she watched as the man ran a hand through his hair before on putting his hat. With a shake of his head, he turned and sauntered down the stairs toward a huge black Chevy Tahoe.

From the top of the stairs, Poppet whispered incredulously, "Who in the world was that handsome gentleman?"

Chapter Seven

Aggie dabbed a thin, flowered paper napkin on her upper lip to blot off the sweat. *Thank God I don't wear make up like I used to,* Aggie thought. The desert military base Jason served on was almost unbearably hot. Near her feet, a beckoning pool shimmered coolly in the late afternoon sun. Umbrella covered tables were placed around the marble patio where people milled about, chatting and visiting.

They all looked so comfortable, even the officers in their full-dress uniforms. She herself wore a light cotton dress, no stockings and tiny sandals, but she glistened like a recently basted turkey in this heat. She glanced at Niddie who looked equally uncomfortable. Niddie's pasty white knees and long, boney legs glowed in the sun while every other pair of legs in view was tan and toned. She had to applaud Niddie for her bravery. Comfort above style. And then there was Poppet.

Poppet was perched on her chair in the long black skirt with elastic waist band and bright white cotton shirt she always wore. The formerly starched shirt was limp and the cloth of the skirt stuck to her skin. Beads of sweat gathered on her forehead but she sat upright and proper. Emptying her third glass of iced tea, she looked around miserably.

"How long do we have to stay?" Niddie hissed around the straw that connected her drink to her lips.

Aggie sniffed. "Settle in. We need to scope out these people. We need to find our next mark before we can go home next week."

Aggie's son, Jason, and his wife had trotted them from party to luncheon to event every day since they arrived here at the base where Jason was stationed. He'd proudly showed them his life and introduced them to the important people with whom he worked. As much as she'd enjoyed seeing her son in his element, Aggie was frankly looking forward to going back home to their quiet life. She was thinking wistfully about the calm farm and the slow pace of their lives when a shadow covered her lap.

"Mother?" Her tall, handsome son stood in front of her in full uniform. Her heart swelled as she looked up at him. "I want you to meet our host."

He reached a hand to her and helped her out of the chair. Behind her, she heard Niddie and Poppet slide out of their chairs as well. An equally tall older man stood at attention next to her boy. "Mother, meet General John McGwire. General, this is my mother Agatha Masterson Hennenfent.

Aggie put her hand out. "Aggie, please. Nice to meet you. These are my sisters, Enid and Prudence."

"Niddie," the oldest sister said automatically as she shook the imposing man's hand.

"I'm Poppet," the last sister said softly.

The officer turned to each woman and formally greeted them. "I'd heard there were three lovely ladies taking my base by storm! I'm so glad you've come to visit our home. I trust it's not too hot for you."

Niddie snorted, feeling like she was baking in her own juices. Poppet sniffed. More graciously, Aggie smiled and said, "I, for one, will be very happy when we get back home. I'm sure this weather is fine for you Desert Dwellers."

The general smirked and launched into a discussion on the benefits of the weather in other places he'd lived. As he spoke, a large black Doberman pinscher slid silently into position at the general's side and dropped on his haunches. Sitting as if at attention, he looked the women over. Aggie, the animal lover, dropped back into her chair.

"Who is this?" She held a hand out to the dog, who sat without a twitch at full attention by the general's side.

"This is Satin, our specially trained guard dog. Satin, at ease."

Immediately, the delicate but well-muscled dog relaxed. He dropped his head and stretched his neck out toward Aggie's proffered hand. Aggie slid her hand over the broad forehead and scratched behind his left ear. He quivered under Aggie's touch and sidled in close enough to put his head in her lap with a deep sigh.

Aggie laughed. "I have to say he doesn't seem like other guard dogs I've known."

"That's because I introduced you to him. When he knows you, he's quite safe in a party situation. He's quite young yet, still a playful pup at heart really." The general snapped his fingers. Satin lifted his head and looked at his master. With a subtle move, the general gestured toward Niddie. Satin immediately moved to a position in front of Niddie. He dropped his bottom back down and regally offered a paw for shaking. Niddie, not usually impressed by animal tricks, took the paw and looked into the deep brown eyes. The dog looked back evenly as if gauging her intentions.

Unnerving, thought Niddie. The general snapped his fingers again and gestured toward Poppet.

"Oh! Oh! No! No!" Poppet pressed herself deeply into the padded chair. She threw her hands over her face. "I don't trust big dogs! They like to bite and hurt people!"

"Satin. Gently." The general ordered. Immediately, Satin dropped to the ground and crawled on his belly toward Poppet. At her feet, he rolled over and waved his huge feet in the air. Poppet peeked out from between her fingers. The sight of the big, dangerous dog lying on his back made her smile. She tentatively reached down and scratched the massive chest. The dog gave a happy groan and wiggled in delight. "See. If he understands you're a guest, he won't hurt you."

"Can I feed him?"

"Here." The general reached into his pocket and pulled out a piece of beef jerky. "He loves these." He snapped his fingers. "Satin. Release." The dog sat up again.

Poppet took the jerky and offered the dried meat to the dog on her open palm. The dog's nose quivered, but he never moved. "Go ahead. Take the treat." Poppet encouraged, but the dog never flinched. A long thread of drool slipped out from the side of the dog's mouth, but he held steady.

The general smiled and then commanded. "Satin, snark!" Immediately, the dog's long tongue snaked out and took the treat.

"He's trained not to take anything from anyone but his handler unless he hears the right command. We always choose a word rarely used in conversation. Because men come and go, animals have to get used to more than one handler and, of course, they might be sold or given away when they get older or if they have a career ending injury. They would have to be destroyed if they'd only eat from one hand. And, for me, that is not acceptable."

"I guess that's a good thing for a guard dog." Aggie said, looking at the beautifully muscled dog who'd returned to his master's side. She was in awe of the dog's intelligence.

Jason informed his aunts and mother. "The general started out in the K-9 units. He has trained dogs for every situation."

The general reached down to scratch the dog's ears. Satin heaved a sigh and leaned against the uniformed legs. "Satin is our finest recruit. I know it's hard to tell, but he's combat trained. My wife didn't want a trained killer in our house with all the guests we have coming in and out all the time or when the grandkids come over. But I still wanted our property to be safe. So we compromised and I designed a new type of training. He's a perfectly behaved family dog. He's been trained to let anyone wander anywhere around the house ... when we're here. If we aren't here, he'll still let anyone come in and move around as they please. He'll never attack or bite unless commanded to do so."

"How does that make him a guard dog? If he doesn't stop robbers from coming in when you're gone?" Aggie asked.

Behind Aggie's back, Niddie raised an eyebrow and looked at Poppet. Poppet's eyes grew big as she looked back at Niddie. She subtly shook her head, but Niddie nodded slowly and raised the other eyebrow. She was sure that Whoodah Thunket would approve of this target!

The general continued, oblivious of the silent conversation going on behind his back. "You might think that, but there's one other part of his training we don't talk about. Only a ..."

At that moment, the general's wife came into view and called out to him. He turned toward her. "Phone, dear. The White House calling."

The general waved a hand and turned back to the sisters. "Duty calls. Please enjoy the rest of your visit. Satin, escort." Satin moved around to sit beside Aggie. "He obviously likes you. He'll stay with you until you leave," the general said as he strode off. Aggie tickled the dog's ears absently.

"You sure made an impression," Jason smiled down at his mother. "I don't think I've ever seen him leave Satin with a guest before."

The general's wife wandered over to where the sisters sat and greeted them. Niddie complimented her on the home. The proud woman immediately insisted they take a tour of the house. With an arrogance shown only by those born of wealth and station, the woman casually pointed out all the valuable paintings and artifacts they'd gathered from the various places they'd been stationed. All three sisters oohed and aahed appropriately while the gushing woman prattled on.

Once back from the tour, Aggie said, "You must spend a lot of time beside this pool. I don't think

I've ever seen such clear beautiful water. Is the pool hard to keep clean?"

The general's wife waved a dismissive hand and offered an explanation while continually scanning the crowd. "Oh, good Heaven's, dearie. I have no idea. The general takes care of all that. All I know is that people come once a week. I have to lock Satin in the house with me and they come through that gate over there. They do what they need to do and then they leave. I don't even see them." Her eyes locked on a woman coming from the house. "Oh, excuse me. I must greet the newcomers."

Aggie watched the woman move through the crowd, leaving a wake of people behind her. She looked down at Satin and tickled his ears. "You know, Satin, I don't think she likes you much. She never even talked to you and you didn't go to her. Poor thing."

At that moment, Satin chose to yawn. His wide mouth showed a bevy of sharp, long teeth. Poppet gasped. "He's really scary when he does that! I think he has more teeth than Satan."

Satin looked at Poppet, winked one eye and settled down on the cool marble for a nap. Poppet laughed. "Maybe he is just a big sweet puppy."

Niddie snorted. "You can trust him if you want to, but I think there's more to him than we know."

"Pshhhawwww, Niddie," Aggie smiled down at the sleeping animal.

Chapter Eight

Later that night, in the large guest suite Jason's wife had set up for them, the sisters sat huddled together talking.

"I think this is a perfect target," Niddie whispered. "I went to the bathroom and stopped by the master bedroom. There's jewelry all over the place and I sincerely doubt the madam would own mere costume stuff. I'd bet big money there's an old safe in the back of the closet," Niddie snickered.

Aggie asked, "Do you think you could get the mechanism open? I doubt the general's the type to leave anything unlocked."

"I already thought of that," Niddie responded confidently. "I bet that thing's much older than you'd think. Probably, a lot like the one Poppa taught me on. More than likely installed when the house was built and not upgraded since. Lord knows how many generals have lived here since the place was built. I don't think I'll have any trouble. If I can't open it, we'll look for something else as valuable and easy to carry. I didn't notice any alarms or cameras or anything."

"They must have a lot of faith in Satin," Aggie said, shaking her head. "I just wish we knew more about the other part of his training the general mentioned."

Poppet nervously asked, "Well - just what will we do about that 'Satan' dog?"

"His name is Satin!" exclaimed Aggie.

"You can call him whatever you want to," Poppet sniffed. "But I know a devil when I see one!"

Niddie broke in to stop the argument. "We'll have to think of something, but the dog followed me around when I was scoping things out and just watched me. I don't think we'll have a problem with him, especially if Aggie works her magic..." Niddie waggled her eyebrows. "... and we bring enough beef jerky."

Poppet sniffed loudly in contempt.

The sisters got ready for bed. Once the lights were out, Aggie whispered, "Jason will never forgive me if we mess this up."

"We won't," Niddie scoffed. "This is a simple job. Besides, who'd ever suspect three little old ladies?

There were lots of other people there and that leaves a lot of possibilities."

Poppet whimpered in the dark. "I just don't like those teeth."

Together Niddie and Aggie growled, "Shut up Poppet!"

"Jason said he and the general are going on something called a bivouac this weekend, like a training camping trip for the young recruits," Niddie reported over breakfast the next morning after Jason and his wife had left for work. "The general doesn't usually go, but he wants to see some of the new dogs working. The timing is perfect. The general's wife is going to visit her grandkids. She was bragging about that at the party so the house should be empty."

"But we're supposed to go home Friday," Poppet whined, "I miss my bed and I'm sure I'm missed at the church."

Niddie rolled her eyes. "We'll tell Jason we decided to take one briefer trip to see those caves he told us about and that way we can wait till he comes back to say good bye. That'll give us a good reason to keep the rental car too."

Aggie nodded, staring at her hands clasped in her lap, but added nothing.

"What's with you?" Niddie asked.

"I'm just not sure about this," Aggie responded. "Putting ourselves at risk is one thing, but endangering Jason's career is another."

Poppet sat up from where she'd been lying on the bed. "I'm worried too. I don't want to risk hurting our Jason ... or seeing that Satan dog!"

"Satin!" hissed the other two sisters in unison.

"Whatever!" Poppet declared. "I just think working around that animal's too dangerous. Remember the general said there was something else no one but he knew about the evil dog's training."

"Come on, Poppet," Niddie chided. "You saw how much Satin loved the treats. We're taking a three-pound bag of all beef jerky. That should be totally enough to keep him busy for quite some time. He'll pay more attention to the jerky than to us going through things. Aggie'll calm him down and you'll keep him interested in the jerky until we finish the job. Then we just give him the rest of the bag of jerky and leave. No one will ever know."

"Just seems too easy to me," Poppet groaned.

Chapter Nine

The three women walked near the head high stone fence that surrounded the general's residence and looked in at the neat one-level house bathed in the light of the early dusk. Anyone would think someone was in the home with all the lights that blazed indoors and out.

"The lights are on too early. They must be on timers," Aggie whispered. Niddie nodded and moved toward the tall iron gate embedded in the middle of the stone wall. Through the iron bars, the gleaming blue pool lay calm and undisturbed. At last weekend's party, the general's wife had pointed out the iron gate that was used by the yard and pool people for access to the area. She had liked the general for the most part, but his wife seemed quite full of herself. She was clear as to what she thought of the help. She didn't even want to see the lowly people who kept her life moving smoothly.

Behind Niddie, Poppet was crowded so close to her sisters that her arms rested on Aggie's shoulders. Aggie kept trying to dust her off but Poppet clung to her like a newborn spider monkey. When Aggie stopped just behind Niddie, the two almost fell in a heap on the ground.

"Get off me! What are you trying to do? Kill us both?" Aggie snapped. "You cannot walk in the same space that I'm walking."

Still trying to snuggle in close to her sister, Poppet looked left and right. "I know that vicious beast is here somewhere. I just want to be close to the one of us he liked best. That way he sees you before he sees me!"

Aggie scoffed at her sister. "Don't be silly! You're the one who has the jerky! He'll smell that and come to you first!"

That thought hadn't occurred to Poppet before. She started to take the pouch off and hand the strap to Aggie. "You take this," she said nervously giggling.

"No," Aggie pushed the pouch back to Poppet. "I'm carrying the tools. We're trusting you with our insurance plan!" She leaned in to Poppet's ear and whispered, "Second chances. Remember?"

Poppet draped the pouch back around her neck and patted the leather pouch reassuringly. *Aggie was right,* she thought. If the crazy dog came at her, she'd just throw that heavy bag at him, yell that eat command, and run like the devil himself were on her heels ... which would be true if the dog didn't stop for the jerky. Poppet gave a small shudder at that thought.

Niddie hushed the bickering the sisters. "I wonder where Satin is?" She mused aloud. All three sisters squeezed in and peeked through the tall iron bars, scanning the darkening yard and empty patio.

"No sign of him," Aggie sighed, "but, with his dark coat, he could be lying in the shadows anywhere, watching us."

When they stepped back from the partially hidden gate, Niddie reached out to slide the latch up, but stopped short. "Look." She pointed to a white sign posted on the edge of the gate just above the latch. Bright red letters stood out in the afternoon light. All three sisters stared.

Aggie began to read softly, "Warning! Silent guard dog on duty!" She looked at Niddie. "Hmm, I wondered why we never heard him bark." She turned back to the sign. "Enter at your own risk. This is a military officer's home.

You have been warned. Should you choose to ignore the warning, you will be prosecuted to the fullest extent of military law before being handed over the the local authorities at the earliest opportunity."

Poppet gasped. "Fullest extent! Military law! Oh, my Heavens, they'll hang us!" She slapped her plump hands to her stricken face and sobbed heavily into them. Aggie wrapped her arms around her shoulders, but Niddie wasn't fazed.

"No, they won't," she sneered at her sobbing sister. "I happen to know that you cannot be punished by the military if you're not in the military. They'd have to hand us over to the local police immediately."

"And that would be better how?" Poppet threw her head up and glared at her older sister from the safety of Aggie's arms. "Besides, just how would you know anything about that? You always think you know everything."

Niddie stood in her usual challenging stance, arms akimbo, one eye brow raised, and stared down her defiant little sister. "Yes ... and how often am I wrong?"

Under the power of Niddie's challenging glare, Poppet had to divert her damp eyes and accept that truth. Niddie was right most of the time, much to Poppet's annoyance.

Exasperated, Niddie continue to explain. "I had to do research on hundreds of topics when I worked in the library. Remember when old Tommy Ducat's kid went AWOL and he was hiding out from the MPs? He asked me to find out the difference between military and local law and when each prevails."

Both sisters stood silently, unable to argue the point.

Aggie continued to comfort Poppet and reassure her. "There, there, Poppet. We won't let you be taken by any authorities, military or local. Niddie won't let us get caught. I'm sure she has a good plan. Just calm down and let's get on with this."

Poppet wiped her eyes with her shirt sleeve and sniffed. She partially turned away from Niddie. For the rest of the long, scary afternoon and evening, she was only going to talk to Aggie, her favorite sister.

Niddie shook her head. She could almost hear the silent conversation in Poppet's head as her sister, once again, decided to ostracize her. Just as well, she thought. Maybe she'd be able to think better without all these constant silly interruptions. Ignoring the sign, she lifted the cool metal handle on the gate. She'd expected a complaining squeak, but heard nothing. Trust the general to insist that his equipment be in perfect working order! She slipped inside and scanned the area again. The sun was setting, but the fading sunlight was still strong enough to have a clear view of the yard. As far as she could see, there was no sign of the dog or anyone else. She leaned back out the gate and called to her sisters, "Come on, girls. Let's get going."

The other two wasted no time slipping inside to join Niddie. As they stood in a huddle, deciding which way to go, Aggie gave a sudden sharp gasp and looked down.

"Oh my! Hello there!" she said softly.

Standing silently at her side was Satin. Niddie froze, but Poppet sidestepped around to Aggie's back with slow, tiny steps, her hands never losing contact with her sister and her eyes never leaving the dog's face.

Bending down to pet the dog, Aggie said, "He must've been in the bushes behind us. He just came up and nudged my hand."

"I'm getting the jerky!" Quickly, Poppet reached for the leather pouch. At her sudden movement,

Satin snapped to attention and shifted around Aggie enough to stare at Poppet intently.

"No!" Both Niddie and Aggie threw their arms out in a protective move to cover their younger sister. Aggie whispered calmly, "Don't make any sudden moves or loud noises." Poppet froze, barely stopping the scream poised on her trembling lips.

Aggie stepped back between Poppet and Satin and said firmly, "Satin! At ease!"

The dog shook himself from head to toe and reluctantly settled back on his haunches. "There! See! He's a good boy," Aggie crooned. She reached down and patted his head again. Not at all reassured at the dog's reaction to Aggie's instruction, Poppet was careful to stay behind her sister.

"You think he'll listen to you the whole time we're here?" Poppet whispered.

"I sure hope so," breathed Aggie.

Niddie turned to face the house and prodded, "We need to get on with this. Let's go." The silent sentry calmly fell into step behind them. At the sliding glass door that led into the house, Niddie reached her hand out. She paused to look down at the dog. Satin stood quietly at Aggie's side watching Niddie with great curiosity. He tipped his head slightly to the left and then to the right, as if asking Niddie what she was going to do next. Aggie's hand rested easily on his head.

"He doesn't seem to be upset with us," Aggie said happily, when Niddie looked at her for further assurance. "I think he remembers us or, at least, me." She nodded at the door and told Niddie, "Go ahead and open the door. See what he does."

Surprised to find the sliding door unlocked, Niddie tugged the glass panel open. As soon as she did, Satin pranced into the room and turned around to wait for them.

Niddie looked at Aggie. "This is the oddest guard dog I've ever seen."

Aggie could only shake her head and agree silently.

Niddie stepped inside and motioned for the others to follow her. Quickly, Poppet slid up close to Aggie, continuing to keep her sister between herself and the prancing dog. She wasn't about to take her eyes off him. They could trust that animal if they wanted to, but Poppet wasn't going to let him sneak up on her. She gently patted the leather pouch to make sure the jerky was still there.

The women walked confidently across the main room and into the hall way. Niddie led them to the master bedroom. Even though she knew there was no one else there, she stopped and looked around before motioning her sisters inside. The huge closet across from the door took up half of the wall space. The louvered doors stood half open. Niddie walked confidently over and pulled the light wooden doors apart.

Inside the dark closet was a perfect example of military precision. All of the long sleeved, pressed shirts were lined up facing the same direction, sorted by color – even though they were all shades of blue. Crisp, formal jackets hung over equally well pressed pants, all lined up as if on parade. No errant lint nor mote of dust dared alight on those shoulders. Below stood a neat line of shiny, spotless shoes. Their heels pressed against the back of the closet. Niddie carefully moved three pair to the side, turned to the left and gestured at a large dark object. The old black safe stood silent sentry in the furthest corner.

"See? Almost exactly like the one Poppa had." She said and knelt down. She held out a hand to Aggie. "Give me the bag." Aggie, who was right behind Niddie, handed the tool satchel to her. As Niddie opened the old scratched, brown bag, she directed Aggie to go and sit on the bed. "Keep Satin with you."

"What should I do ... AGGIE?" Poppet said pointedly, making sure Niddie knew she still wasn't talking to her.

Aggie told her sister to go out in the hall and act as look out ... just in case. Poppet hesitated. "Why? There's no one here. Are you worried?"

With a shake of her head, Aggie continued, "We just need someone out there in case. You never know."

Poppet nodded. "Promise me you'll warn me before you come out so I can be far out of ..." Poppet gestured at Satin. "... that thing's way."

"Don't be silly. He's a good boy, aren't you, Satin?" The big dog looked adoringly at Aggie and tried to lay a big sloppy lick on her cheek, but missed and got her neck. Aggie laughed and wiped the moisture off with the back of her hand. But Poppet wasn't impressed.

"Ha! He's not fooling me! He's just cleaning off a place to bite!" Poppet turned quickly and went out of the room. Behind her, she heard Aggie cooing to the beast. Better her than me, thought Poppet, as she closed the door.

Chapter Ten

Bored, Poppet leaned against the wall in the hallway. She'd already looked at all the pictures and walked the length of the hall twice. She was tired of waiting. Her watch said she'd been out there about 15 minutes when she heard a double gasp from inside the bedroom. Poppet slowly opened the wooden door and looked to where her sisters were huddled inside the closet. Satin poised over the hunched women, but he turned when the door opened.

"What happened?" she quizzed.

"Stay there. We're almost done," Aggie said.

"But I don't want to ..." Poppet started to argue when she saw Satin shift his attention to her. She stuck her tongue out at the dog and watched as he licked his lips. Then she slowly withdrew and closing the door quietly.

Two minutes later, the two older sisters came out of the bedroom with their silent guardian trotting on their heels.

"Did you find anything?" Poppet asked.

With a bemused look on her face, Niddie shook her head.

"Nothing?" demanded Poppet. "You found nothing! All this for nothing?!"

Aggie patted her arm. "We found diamonds. Lots and lots of uncut diamonds. Just the kind Poppa used to bring home."

Poppet's jaw dropped. She looked at Niddie who nodded and said, "We only took about half of them though. That should be plenty for what we need."

Poppet was as surprised as her sisters. "That's great!"

Niddie nodded. "We need to get out of here. Now! Let's go."

They walked quietly back down the hall and started across the living room, when something crossed Aggie's mind. "Niddie? Do we know anyone who can sell them for us?" Niddie stopped dead in her tracks, so quickly that both Aggie and Poppet crashed into her. Barely staying on her feet, she snarled, "Let's just get out of here. We'll worry about that later."

Niddie approached the sliding door they had left slightly open when they entered. As she reached for the handle, Satin stepped between her and the glass. Niddie heard a low growl. Satin's lips were curled back in a silent warning.

Niddie took her hand off the door handle, stepped back a pace and motioned to her sister. "Uhm, Aggie? Your friend seems to be a little bit upset."

"I'll get him. At ease, Satin!" The dog relaxed a little, but not as much as he had on the patio. "Satin! At ease!" Aggie commanded more firmly. The dog moved aside a bit, started to drop to his haunches, but then stayed on his feet. "Satin, come here." Aggie snapped her fingers. With one more look at Niddie, Satin walked over to Aggie and sat down beside her.

"OK, you and Poppet go outside."

Niddie opened the door and Poppet wasted no time pushing Niddie out of her way and stepping through the door first. "Poppet!"

But Poppet was already on her way to the other side of the pool. Niddie stepped outside. Even though the quivering dog stayed at Aggie's side, she used her legs to block the opening.

"Try to keep him inside." Niddie said as she waited for her sister to come through.

Aggie nodded her agreement.

"Satin! Stay!" She waved a finger at the dog, moved to the door and slipped through. As soon as she stepped out, Satin jumped at the door, but the glass stopped him. He dropped to his haunches and regarded her through the glass like she'd betrayed him. After a few seconds, he jumped up and disappeared into the kitchen.

"Well, that was easy enough," Aggie smiled, dusting off her hands. At that moment, the women heard a loud clattering of toe nails on the marble patio and saw the huge figure of the dog charging around the corner.

Aggie looked at Niddie. Niddie looked back. Simultaneously, the sisters said, "Pet door!"

"I should've thought of that," Aggie said, shaking her head.

"Yeah, you should have, *Dog Lover*." Sarcasm dripped from Niddie's words. Her disappointment was clear.

"I'm not so sure about him anymore, Niddie."

"Well, that's not a good thing. Aggie, you said you could make him behave."

Aggie defended herself. "He's been well behaved up until now. I think we should just go to the gate and leave. Maybe slip him a piece or two of jerky and then go."

Niddie considered the dog sitting between them and the iron gate. Bright eyes watched them while his pink tongue hung out like a puppy hoping for a game of fetch. Dammed if the dog didn't seem to be enjoying this little game they were playing, she thought. Aggie was right. He really hadn't tried to hurt them. Except for that one little growling thing at the door, he seemed perfectly happy just to hang with them. Niddie gathered herself up and said, "OK. Let's see what happens. Poppet, get some jerky ready. We're going to walk to the gate and leave."

Poppet nodded, pulled the big bag out of her pouch and tore the top open. Several pieces fell to the ground. Satin looked at them with interest, but didn't make a move toward them.

"Leave them there," Niddie commanded. "Maybe, when we get closer, he'll smell them and ignore us."

Calmly, Aggie and Niddie walked toward where Poppet stood. Poppet bravely watched the big animal follow in her sisters' footsteps. She didn't know what she'd do if he suddenly began to eat her sisters. The mere thought of that made her hands shake and her eyes teared up.

"Walk faster. I'm getting really scared," she pleaded.

"Stay calm," Aggie said softly. "He won't get upset unless you do."

"I certainly hope so," Poppet wasn't buying that reasoning though. To her, that dog looked like he was up to something. Something no good.

Niddie and Aggie walked past the slightly quivering Poppet. Aggie grabbed Poppet's arm, steadying her, and said, "Just drop the pieces like Hansel and Gretel did when they went into the woods."

Poppet's lip quivered, "I always hated that fairy tale!" She looked down at the dog. He'd sniffed at a piece or two, but didn't touch any. He was drooling like he had before, but he wasn't paying any attention to the dropped meat after the first sniff.

Poppet's voice quivered. "I don't think he's going to let us leave. He's not stopping to eat the meat!"

"I see that," Niddie said. "Aggie?"

"Just keep on walking. He seems fine. Only a few more feet." The women linked arms and stepped off the edge of the marble patio on to the manicured lawn on a slow journey toward the exit, carefully deliberate step after another.

Just as they were halfway to the gate, Satin launched his powerful body into the air and landed between them and the safety of the portal.

"Holy Mary, Mother of God!" exclaimed Poppet. Her whole body began to shake.

"Steady," Niddie's voice was in her ear. "Aggie, see if he'll come to you."

Aggie let go of her sisters' arms and bent down. She held her hand out and chirped to the semi-crouching dog. "Come here, you good boy. Come to Aggie."

The dog's lip was curled back and a low growl came menacingly from his throat. Aggie jerked upright.

"Ok! Ok! We need to think this out," Niddie cautioned. "He didn't get upset until we stepped off the concrete. Go back to the patio and we'll just sit down on those chairs and think this part out."

Without turning their backs on the alert but calm animal, the women edged to the patio. All three slowly sagged into the nearby canvas chairs and regarded the still vigilant dog. Satin stood quietly and waited. When they didn't move, Satin sat down on the grass between them and the gate and regarded the three women in return.

"I wonder if that's the last part of his training," Niddie thought aloud.

"What?" Aggie asked.

"Maybe he's trained to let anyone in, but then NOT let anyone out. That way he'll hold the burglars here until someone comes home."

With hands clenched, Poppet started her favorite mantra for scary situations. "Ohhh, whatawegonnado! Whatawegonnado?"

Satin leapt to his feet.

Both sisters hissed, "Shut up, Poppet!"

"Shhhhh. it's ok, darlin'," Aggie whispered to the dog. "At ease, Satin." Satin slowly eased back down to the ground.

The women sat in silence, listening to insects whine in the distance. A bull frog croaked in the grass. The only other sounds were that of the dog's breathing and Poppet's sniffing. Aggie wondered if fireflies could live in the dry hot climate. She shook the errant thought out of her head. She had much more important things to be concerned about at this minute. Then Niddie put her hands on the arms of the white wicker chair and heaved a determined sigh.

"Ok, here is what we're going to do," Niddie announced, taking charge again. "We need to distract him with the jerky and make a run for safety. And I do mean run! No matter how much your legs or back hurts. We'll rest on the other side of the gate."

The two younger sisters nodded in agreement.

"Ok, stand up – slowly." They stood easily so as not to excite the dog ... and Satin matched their movement. He lowered his head, but didn't growl. Aggie thought she could see his stub of a tail wagging in the gloaming.

"I honestly think he sees this as a game for us to play. He's enjoying himself," said Aggie.

"Well, make him stop," hissed Poppet in a low voice. "A game is only fun when everyone likes playing."

"Let me try one more time," said Aggie.

"Fine, but be careful," Niddie cautioned.

"Be VERY careful," added Poppet.

Aggie stepped forward and clucked at the dog. "Come on, Satin. At ease. You remember me, your old pal, Aggie. You don't want to bite me. We're friends." Aggie took two tentative steps forward. As soon as she stepped off the marble, the dog began moving his mouth like he was barking. The astonished women watched as the dog's straining jaw moved, but not a sound came out. Then, suddenly, Satin lifted a front paw and stomped the ground between them.

That was the last straw for Poppet. She screamed loudly and threw her hands up over her head. She knocked over her chair and ran toward the pool. Satin, ready to play more of this new game, trotted after her. He didn't move fast enough to be chasing her, but was soon within reach of her flying feet.

Aggie took off after them. "Poppet! Stop! Satin! Attention! Poppet!"

With a loud gasp, Niddie took off adding her cries to Aggie's.

Poppet's blind fear of the dog didn't allow her to hear her sisters. Between gasps of air, Poppet screamed, "Help me! Help me!" With every other step, she threw a handful of jerky over her shoulder at the loping dog. He ignored the little meat bombs, continuing behind her, tongue hanging out, gaily giving chase. Poppet kept running, her hands alternately flailing in the air over her head and tossing handfuls of jerky over her shoulder.

Aggie raced after them, gasping and yelling, "Stop, Poppet! Don't run! He thinks you're playing."

"Satin! Attention!" bellowed Niddie, hot on Aggie's heels, already breathing heavily.

"Help me!" Poppet screamed. "He's going to eat me!"

"He thinks you're playing, Poppet," yelled Aggie. "Stop!"

The little panic parade had circled the pool once and already the breathless women knew this had to stop and soon. The dog was having the time of his life, but they couldn't keep this up much longer.

Aggie and Niddie stopped and bent over, gasping for air. They watched the dog follow Poppet and noticed the only time he threatened her was when she was near the gate. Even then, he just shouldered her away from the exit. Poppet screamed louder and tried to move faster when she felt the dog at her side.

Gasping, Niddie called to Aggie. "She's going to have a heart attack. Or maybe I will! We need to stop her!" All Aggie could do was nod and step in front of Poppet. Poppet crashed into Aggie, but continued trying to run from the dog. Niddie grabbed her as well. The two older sisters held Poppet tight enough to make her settle down a bit. "Breathe, Poppet," yelled Aggie. "Breathe!"

Slowly, Poppet realized the dog had dropped into the grass and lay there watching the three women. His tongue lolled out and there was a happy grin on his face. He was ready to go again as soon as they were.

Aggie noticed the jerky strewn all over the pool deck. Why wasn't the dog stopping to eat his favorite treat, she wondered. That's when Aggie remembered that Satin needed that command to eat. She turned to her older sister.

"Niddie! I'll get his attention. You slip over to the gate and get ready." She huffed out the words. She heard Niddie's muffled affirmation.

"Poppet, stay here and be calm," Poppet nodded.

"Satin. Come here, baby. That's a good boy. Come to me." Aggie crooned to the happy animal. He stood as if trying to decide whether he was going to go to her or not. After several seconds of deliberation, he pranced over to her. Aggie grabbed his collar and began rubbing him all over and praising him. All the while she talked, she turned his head away from the gate. Niddie slipped through the opening and stood outside the gate.

Aggie looked at Poppet. "OK. Give me the jerky." The red-faced, panting Poppet handed her the half empty bag. "Now!" Aggie tightened her hold on the collar and drew in a deep breath. "We're going to walk around the pool toward the gate. When we get to the gate again, I'll start running and Satin will chase me. You run as fast as you can to Niddie."

Poppet glanced toward where Niddie stood with the gate at the ready. Poppet gulped and nodded.

Aggie called out. "Come on, Satin. Let's play this game, good boy." She reached down and patted the big head at her hip. The two women walked easily with the dog right behind them. As they came level with the gate, Aggie whispered "go now!" to Poppet and "Come on Satin" to the dog. She took off running with Satin bouncing on her heels. She heard the iron gate slam when Poppet was safe and knew she was on her own. She just had to keep the dog distracted one more trip around the pool.

In the meantime, she had to think of the word that would make the dog stop and pick up the morsels. The lack of oxygen getting to her belabored lungs made thinking hard but she tried to focus.

She dropped a few pieces of jerky and yelled anything she could think of that might make the dog stop. She knew the command started with an S.

"Satin! Snake!" No, that wasn't the command. The dog pranced alongside her. She tried a new word with every few steps.

"Satin! Snail!" Nothing!

What was that word?

"Satin! Snipe!" Curses!

"Satin! For Heaven's sake, stop!" Satin happily shook his head as he pranced along.

Nearly blind with exhaustion, Aggie rounded the last turn of the pool before the gate. She could see her sisters waving her on and yelling, but the blood was pounding so loud in her ears she couldn't hear them.

Then, out of the blue, she remembered! She dropped the nearly empty bag of jerky, stopped dead still, and yelled, "Satin! Snark!"

Instantly, the dog skidded to a stop. He looked at Aggie, tipped his head side to side and then looked at the gate. Much to Aggie's surprise, he turned his back, trotted to the pool deck, dropped his massive head and began slurping up the meat chunks, drops of drool flying in every direction.

"Run, Aggie!" Niddie called out. Niddie held the gate slightly open. Aggie took off for the opening as fast as her exhausted legs would carry her. She fell through the escape that her sister made for her, into welcoming arms. Niddie slammed the gate closed and they all sank to the damp grass, gasping for air. Almost immediately, the sisters heard a loud thud. Niddie had closed the gate just in time for Satin to crash head long into the metal bars.

Aggie stayed wrapped in her sisters' arms, breathing heavily. On the other side of the gate, Satin sat with a bemused look on his face. He seemed to have taken quite a blow when he hit the metal barrier. He stared at the women for a few minutes. Then he stood, shook his massive head, walked back to the pool deck and began vacuuming the jerky from the patio.

"He's gonna have such a bad belly ache in the morning," Poppet mused out loud.

Chapter Eleven

"Ok, here's the deal," Niddie gathered her sisters around the kitchen table. Aggie had shared a letter from her daughter, Christine. "We go down to Christine's house and open the place up for them. If we go next week, we can spend a couple of weeks getting the house ready, enjoying the sunshine and finding our next mark."

Poppet squirmed in her chair. "How much more do we need? I don't want to keep doing this!"

Niddie looked at her sister and said, "You can stay here if you want. No one's forcing you to go to the land of warm sunshine, beaches, and palm trees. Look at all that snow on the ground. You can stay and save us the money we'd pay the Johnson twins to see to the animals."

Poppet started to say something, but Aggie chimed in. "Don't start agitating her, Niddie. We aren't leaving her here. We're in this together – all or none!"

"Yeah," Poppet sniffed. "Besides you're not cheating me out of a warm winter vacation!"

WHOOOOOOOOSH!

All three women shuddered. The windows rattled and the walls shook!

Niddie cursed under her breath.

Aggie wrapped her arms around herself and whispered, "They're getting closer and closer. I can almost smell the cordite!"

Aggie'd done some sniffing around and discovered that Poppet's story of a large mining company searching for deposits in the area was correct. Apparently, many of the big mining companies were returning to previously rejected areas across the country with new technology that made finding hidden deposits easier. No damage had been done as of yet; however, everyone, from the hens to the humans, were disconcerted at the loud blasts that came at inconsistent intervals throughout the day.

Niddie called up the stairs. “Hurry up, Poppet! The cab’s coming down the lane!” Without waiting for an answer, Niddie lugged a pair of heavy suitcases to the front porch where Aggie stood in the brisk air, watching the yellow vehicle racing down the lane.

“Lord,” Aggie said, looking at the bags. “You’d think we were going to Europe for a year.” Niddie dropped the bags with a heavy clunk and gasped.

“I just don’t know what to bring,” Niddie said. She yelled over her shoulder. “Poppet! Get down here!”

From behind them came a muffled voice. “I’m here.”

Aggie gasped when she turned around and saw her younger sister standing in the doorway. Niddie put her hands on her hips and shook her head. There stood Poppet wrapped in her winter coat. Under her coat, she wore several other layers. Aggie could see parts of two sweaters and maybe three shirts sticking out at the collar, hem and sleeves of the coat. On Poppet’s head was a brown felt cap with fur ear flaps. A bright red scarf draped around her neck. On her feet were heavy muckaluck boots.

“What in the Super Sam Hill are you wearing?” Niddie demanded.

"The air's cold. The trip to the airport will be cold." Poppet blew against the fur collar of her coat that half covered her mouth. "You can freeze if you want to, but I'll be nice and toasty."

Niddie stepped toward her sister, saying, "Get some of that stuff off! You'll be miserable and you'll complain the whole time. You probably won't even fit in the plane seat."

Poppet put both hands out and began slapping at Niddie, yelping like a frightened pup suddenly grabbed by the neck. Niddie tried to catch her hands. Like a pair of pre-teen girls, they slapped at each other, Poppet squealing and Niddie muttering under her breath. With a disgusted sigh, Aggie stepped in and stopped the impending row.

"Girls! For pity sakes! The cab's here! We don't have time for this," Aggie finished up.

WHOOOOSH! BOOM!

Poppet jumped toward Niddie and almost knocked her to the ground. All three turned and looked in the direction of the blast as the cab pulled up to the porch. The driver stepped out, leaving the engine running, and nodded at the ladies.

"That was a loud one," the cabbie exclaimed. A white cloud burst from his mouth with each word as he stepped up on the porch to get the bags. He looked at Poppet and smirked, "We'll be lucky to get you stuffed into the back seat!"

Niddie stepped to her sister's defense. "We don't need any of your smart mouth, Dougie Thompson! Just get those bags loaded!" Niddie'd known Dougie since he was in kindergarten. He reacted to her librarian voice as if he were still in grade school.

"Yes, ma'am!" The cabbie sheepishly ducked his head and carried the bags to the car. He couldn't resist watching over his shoulder while Poppet tottered cautiously down the stairs to the cab. She was just about there when ...

WHOOOSH! BOOM!

Another blast ripped the air. He never would've believed that the bundled up little woman could move so quickly. Poppet made her way to the cab, opened the back door, and dove inside with only minimal help from her sisters. Unable to stop the smirk from coming to his lip, Dougie closed the trunk and saw Miss Niddie giving him the angry librarian look over the rim of her glasses. She didn't need to say anything more to send him ducking into the driver's seat without a word. Niddie and Aggie crowded into the back seat on either side of their overstuffed sister.

On the long ride to the airport, Aggie asked, "By the way, did you read the letter that oil company sent you?"

"No!" Niddie said adamantly. "And I'm not going to."

Aggie sighed. "Maybe you should, Sister. I mean, that man did say he had good news for you?"

Niddie scoffed. "Good news? And what might that be? That they're taking part of the farm? That they're going to start drilling on our land whether we like it or not? That we have to take a pittance for the acres we don't even want to sell? Or we can stay but they'll be drilling in the garden next? No thank you!"

Aggie shook her head. Getting around Niddie's stubbornness had always been a challenge. The sisters would have to let her cool down and start thinking logically again. That could take quite some time.

"Not trying to upset you or anything, but he's very handsome." Poppet said from deep inside the pile of clothes between the other two.

"So!?" Niddie glared.

Aggie came to Poppet's rescue. "Niddie, dear, be calm. When we were in town yesterday, we ran into him."

"You did NOT talk to him!" Niddie glared looking back and forth between the two other women. "Tell me you didn't listen to his drivel!"

Poppet snuggled further into the pile of clothes to avoid her angry sister's glare. "No, he wanted to but Aggie said no. She said we'd only talk to him when you were ready and we were all together."

Niddie sniffed, turned to look out window and thought about the landscape she'd loved since she was a child. The barn may be on the verge of collapse now but, in her mind, the building held so many memories of better times. She shook her head slightly and turned back to regard her sisters.

"But ..." Poppet whispered. "... he's very handsome and he did ask about you." She paused for effect and looked at Aggie, then back at Niddie. "He asked, and I quote ..." Poppet made air quotes as best she could. "... how our beautiful sister was." Poppet and Aggie waited for an explosion. Niddie sat completely still for several long seconds.

"Hrumpf!" Niddie snorted and said, "Hopefully, when we get back, he'll be ... uhm, I mean, they'll be done and gone."

Chapter Twelve

Aggie stepped out of the cab and looked at the house her daughter owned. A small whistle of approval escaped her lips. Just behind her shoulder, she felt Niddie's presence.

"That is just plain gorgeous," the older sister whispered.

"Is someone going to help me or what?" came Poppet's whining voice. Still dressed in a thick coat, heavy boots, and the ugly earflap hat, Poppet groaned as she tried to heave her body out the door of the cab. "The temperature must be a million degrees here!"

Aggie reluctantly turned from the view to help her sister. "I told you not to wear so many clothes! How many sweaters do you have on under that coat?" Aggie took one arm and Niddie the other. Between the two, they squeezed their sister out into the sunshine.

"You both complained about the weather all the way to the airport," Poppet whimpered.

Aggie went to the back of the cab to pay the driver and pick up her bags. Poppet followed her to retrieve her own suitcase. They lugged them to the sidewalk and set them down. The long, low, rambling house was just too beautiful not to spend a few moments admiring.

Niddie joined them and said in astonishment, "Have you ever seen anything this beautiful? Why haven't we ever come here before?"

"Christine told me about the oceanside home her husband had inherited," Aggie stood in awe, "but she never told me how big the place was."

Aggie walked down the cobbled sidewalk to the white, single story house that sprawled out in front of them. Niddie paid the driver and grabbed her bags from the curb. She followed Aggie, feeling like a rubber-necking rube who'd never been off the farm. There was so much to see. Beautiful flowering bushes lined the front of the house. The scent of tropical flowers drifted by on the gentle breeze. There was even a topiary of a unicorn at the corner of the lot. A stone fountain sparkled gaily in the sunshine as if inviting birds to come in for a bath.

Poppet stayed at the curb, slowly removing her coat, the hat and scarf as she scanned the groomed yard. She heaved a sigh of relief at the loss of heavy clothing and looked at the house for the first time. Her jaw dropped, as she noticed the view through the house to the ocean. "So much glass!" she gasped. "Who keeps everything so clean?"

She followed her sisters to the ornate blue wooden door just as Aggie slipped the key Christine had sent her into the lock and pushed the door open. Cautioning her sisters to wait, she stepped inside and disappeared behind the door. A few seconds later, she beckoned them in.

"Wow," she said. "This alarm is more complicated looking than the controls in a space capsule!" Turning from the control panel, she saw the looks on her sisters' faces and followed their gazes. Warm honey-colored hard wood floor stretched from stark wall to pristine white wall. The back of the room was floor to ceiling windows with an unobstructed view of the pool and the ocean beyond that.

"Look at all that glass!" Niddie's jaw nearly hit the ground. "I didn't know they made sheets of glass that big." She walked toward the giant windows like a sleepwalker.

Beyond the window lay a glistening blue infinity pool that blended into the distant horizon. The calm ocean breeze gently stirred the branches of the palm trees. The horizon beyond seemed to stretch forever. Puffy white clouds scudded across the deep azure sky. To make the view picture perfect, several small sailboats drifted jauntily along on the freshening breeze.

"My! My! My!" was all Aggie could manage.

Poppet was still frozen in the foyer, awestruck. After admiring the amazing room and view for several minutes, she began sloughing off the rest of the bulky clothes at an alarming rate and letting them fall to the floor at her feet. When she stepped out of the pile, Poppet turned to the right and walked down the broad hall that ran along the front of the house.

Stopping short of the windows, Niddie turned to the left and began to explore the side rooms. Aggie heard doors opening and closing on either side of her as she began carefully pulling the dust cover off a sofa trying not to launch any offending dust into the air.

Poppet's delighted voice echoed down the hall. "You'll never believe this," she shouted. "I've counted four bedrooms and five bathrooms ... and I see another whole house out by the pool!"

"I found the kitchen," Niddie yelled. "I've seen professional kitchens with fewer gadgets in them." She stuck her head around the corner and looked at Aggie. "Come and see this!"

Aggie shook her head and plopped herself down on the overstuffed sofa. The view was enough to take anyone's breath away. In all her life, she'd never seen so many shades of blue other than in a painting. She sighed and wished her late husband, Jeremy, was here to share the romantic view. She let herself dwell in that sorrow for a few moments before shaking off the feeling and rising to meet her sisters as they reappeared near the middle of the great room where she sat.

Poppet plopped down on a large chair without bothering to move the dust cover. Aggie was surprised to see that very little dust rose. That seemed odd to her. The house had been closed up for more than a year. There should be a thick coat of dust on everything. She stood up, walked over to a sideboard and ran a finger across the top. Only the smallest bit of dust was anywhere to be seen. She knit her brows in consternation. *Very odd,* she thought.

"Look at this," Niddie'd come to stand next to her. She held a cream-colored envelope with the word 'Mom' written across the front. Niddie handed the envelope to Aggie without another word.

Aggie opened the thick flap. Inside was a heavy card with her daughter and son-in-law's names on the top in brown ink. Brown ink on cream colored paper, mused Aggie. Trust Christine to add that touch of elegance.

> *Dear Mom and aunties, welcome to my home. If you're reading this, you probably have noticed by now there's not much dust in the place. The truth is I didn't invite you down to open the house. In fact, you'll meet Damian and Johanna on Thursday. They come once a week and do all the housekeeping and yard work for us. I just wanted you to come and enjoy the weather and the sunshine for a month. I knew you wouldn't just come. You three would have to have a purpose. So your*

> *purpose is to enjoy yourself. The house is yours to use as your own. We'll be home in about four weeks. Then you can spend a week with us before traipsing back home to all that snow and ice. You should have the car keys on the ring I sent you. Feel free to use the BMW. Or, if you get to feeling frisky, take the Jag for a spin. And there are bathing suits in the little cabana. -- Love, Christine.*

"Well, that child," Aggie gasped out loud. "My wonderful, thoughtful child." Wiping a tear from her eye, she looked out the window at the little house on the end of the pool. That little cabana was nearly as big as their house at home.

Poppet asked, "Is something wrong?"

Aggie explained what Christine had done. Both Niddie and Poppet stared, aghast at the news. After a few minutes to digest the meaning of the note, Poppet stood up and went back down the hall. "Well, I'm choosing my bedroom first. I want the one with the big TV." She disappeared, leaving a happily whistled tune in the air behind her.

"She's a great kid, that niece of mine," Smiling, Niddie sat down, unsure what to do with herself next. If they were going to stay here, what would they do with themselves for four whole weeks? She looked at her sister. "So what do you want to do now?"

Chapter Thirteen

Aggie shook her head. "I guess we need to pick our bedrooms, see about dinner, and let tomorrow take care of itself."

"Poppet!" Niddie yelled. "Come get your things out of the hall way."

The sound of bare feet slapping against the tile drew their attention. Poppet emerged from the hallway clad in a brightly striped beach towel.

"What's she doing?" gasped Aggie as she took Niddie's arm.

Poppet looked at her astounded sisters. She lifted her chin arrogantly as if defying them to make a comment. "I tried all the suits on and none of them fit me." She took several steps toward the pool but paused once more as if daring herself to go on.

Niddie's jaw dropped but neither she nor Aggie said anything. Poppet waited for a remark from her stunned sisters. When none came, she lifted her chin a bit higher and hiked up the towel a little tighter under her plump arms. "Besides there's no one around here for miles and I'm not wasting another minute of pool time."

With that, Poppet walked purposely toward the pool, each defiant step causing her ample flesh to shudder. At the edge of the pool, she dropped the towel. For a few brief seconds, the light glowed brilliantly off the parts of Poppet that had never seen the sun before. Without another second's hesitation, Poppet stepped off the edge into the glorious cool water.

At the sound of a huge splash, Aggie looked at Niddie in astonishment. The bewildered Niddie glanced out at the pool. With an impish grin, she looked back at Aggie and said, "Looks like Poppet decided what she wants to do. I think I might take a dip too – with a suit on!"

Aggie snorted in laughter. "Me, too, but we definitely need to get her a suit next time we're in town."

Aggie sat opposite Niddie with Poppet next to her in the little sidewalk café they found in the picturesque little town. A gentle breeze scented with a gentle floral aroma wafted past her nose. *January!* She thought. *We're eating breakfast outdoors at a side walk café in mid winter. Amazing.*

"I'm glad you suggested this, Aggie," Niddie said. "I don't think I could've sat around and watched Johanna doing all the work."

"I know," Aggie responded. "I watched Damian pull that lawn equipment off the truck and had a hard time not going out to help dig up weeds or something. They're absolute dynamos!"

"I want waffles! Big golden Belgian waffles," Poppet laughed. As usual, her concerns were different than her sister's.

"We need to decide what we're going to do here," Niddie stage whispered. Even though there was no one else near them, she looked over her shoulder.

Poppet put her menu down with a hard slap and said, "Can't we have just one morning without you bringing up our impending crime spree?" She stared at Niddie with disgust.

"I was talking about the 'touristy' kind of things, Poppet," Niddie retorted. "Like going for a sail boat ride or art museums and other things."

Feeling very small for jumping to conclusions, Poppet picked her menu up with a tiny "Oh" and hid her red face behind the laminated pages.

Aggie tried to lighten the mood again. "I think that a boat ride would be fun. I wonder if there are any fancy houses we can tour. Maybe we should get a newspaper."

At that moment, the waitress came out to take their orders. Before she could leave, Niddie asked how they could find some attractions to go visit. The girl was a well spring of information from having lived in that town all her life. In the middle of her suggestions, the door to the restaurant across the street opened and several young people spilled out laughing and stumbling. The waitress snorted disdainfully.

Poppet whispered. "Are they drunk? This early in the morning?"

With another disgusted sniff, the waitress answered, "No, they're stoned."

"Stoned?" Aggie gasped.

"Yeah, they changed the state laws so people can buy marijuana and then someone opened the pot shop around the corner. We see them all the time." She stood with her hands on her hips and a tight grimace on her lips watching the laughing group disappear around the corner. “Fortunately, they know better than to come in here acting like that.”

“You can buy that stuff here, like you’d buy milk or bread?” Niddie queried incredulously.

The waitress shook her head. “It’s not quite that easy. You have to go to a doctor and get a diagnosis of a specific disease. Then you get an ID card from the state and then you can buy some, but only in small amounts and from licensed sellers. In some states, anyone can buy anything they want, but not here. Not yet.”

Aggie wondered, “So, if you can only get small amounts, how did they get so ... uhm ... hmmm ... affected?”

Once again, the waitress sniffed, “Some people have a real need, like those with glaucoma or cancer. But these kids ... they get some Dr. Feel Good to write them prescriptions that say they have PTSD or anxiety disorder or some other problem whose existence is hard to prove. Then they pool their allotment. Sometimes they smoke the weed and sometimes they put pot into food, like brownies.”

Poppet’s eyes lit up. “Brownies!”

“Steady,” Aggie said, putting a hand on her sister’s arm.

Chapter Fourteen

Lying around the pool in the warm sun, Aggie felt like she'd died and gone to heaven. After a week of having nothing to do, this life was getting easier and easier to feel OK about.

"Aggie," her older sister interrupted her reverie. "We have to decide what we're going to do. Time's slipping away." Niddie sat up and threw her feet off the lounge chair. "I mean, we don't know anyone. How are we going to figure out what house to go to and what to look for? Even if we can get what we think the diamonds are worth, we're still short about $50,000."

Aggie sat up and watched Poppet flopping around in the pool. "Not to start another argument but have you thought any more about the oilman's comments?"

"No." Niddie snapped. "But ..." she said conspiratorially, "... I have thought about that Marlboro Man!"

"Enid Grace!" Aggie laughed at her sister's blush.

Niddie stared off into the distance. "I have to admit, once I got over being mad, I thought about how handsome he is." She turned to face Aggie. "Do you have any idea how few men I have EVER had to look up at?"

Aggie laughed loud enough to make Poppet turn and look in their direction. She waved and watched as Poppet continued to swim.

"I'm so glad you got her into a suit!" Niddie stated.

"Believe me, I had a hard time," Aggie's voice was light with laughter. "But when certain parts got sunburned, the task suddenly became easier." Niddie laughed at the memory of her poor sister's all over sunburn all over her body that first day.

Poppet had never been in a pool before this trip but, since that first dip, she'd hardly left the water. She'd even started lobbying to turning the old barn into an indoor swimming pool.

Aggie nodded at Poppet and said, "Her skin's going to be permanently puckered up before we leave!"

Niddie snickered, "The exercise is good for her and she's happy. We're going to be lucky to get her out of the pool when we leave though." Aggie smiled and nodded. "And about the Marlboro Man ..."

"Enough about the Marlboro Man," Niddie stated flatly.

Aggie giggled at her older sister's discomfort. She had to admit this was fun ... seeing Miss Niddie so completely unsettled and by a man no less.

"Seriously, Aggie, we need a plan."

"I know," Aggie sighed. "I've been wracking my brain. There are lots of houses around but, like you said, how do we figure out what's in them? No one seems to give parties so there's no reason to drop by." She laid back and put her sunglasses on. "I haven't come up with anything yet, but I do have one idea that might help."

Niddie waited for her sister to continue.

"This is Friday. I think we should get dressed up and go to the Antelope Club. I noticed one when I did a web search the other day."

"Antelope Club? What on earth is that?" Niddie questioned.

"Jeremy belonged to the group," Aggie smiled wistfully. "They're all over the world. They started out as men's only clubs, like the Elks, Moose, or Shriner's. They were originally a place where men could be away from their families and drink and carry on. But, in the past few years, they've grown into benevolent groups who do good things for their communities as well as being a social club. Everywhere we went, we'd always check in with the club. Amazingly, we nearly always ran into some one we knew." Aggie sat up again. She took her glasses off and looked at her sister. "Who knows ...?"

Niddie smiled. She hadn't gotten dressed up for a long time. "Well," she stood. "I guess we'd better go shopping then because the one thing I didn't bring was fancy dancing duds."

Chapter Fifteen

Shopping in a small town meant going to the main street and wandering from shop to shop.

"This reminds me of a time before malls came to be," Niddie mused. "I love all these little shops."

Poppet said, "Uh oh, look there." She pointed across the street to the café near where they'd had breakfast the day before. Laughter came from a noisy group of people coming out of the café. They each carried a white Styrofoam box. Some of them were eating the contents with their fingers. Some of them were laughing so hard they staggered against each other, nearly falling down. They wandered down the street and disappeared around the corner.

"Do you think they're ..." Poppet dropped her voice into a whisper. "... stoned?"

"Yes, Poppet," Niddie answered, disgust coloring her words. "Really! Behaving like that in public."

Aggie shook her head as they watched another group stagger out of a coffee shop further up the street and said, "I must admit that I'm a bit curious about the pleasure they find in being so silly. They look like they can barely control their bodies."

She started to walk toward the corner where the rowdy bunch had turned.

"Where are you going?" Poppet whined. "I want to try these pastries." Poppet gestured toward the bakery window behind her.

"You can wait here or come with me. I just want to see what this shop looks like." Aggie walked purposefully across the street, leaving her sisters to follow or not as they would.

While Niddie waited for her, Poppet ducked into the bakery and returned a few moments later with a fragrant box tied with ribbon. As soon as Poppet reached Niddie's side, Niddie grabbed her arm and pulled the grumbling Poppet behind her. They walked quickly to the corner of the block.

When they turned the corner, Aggie was seated on a bench in the morning sun, staring at a building with a green cross glowing on its front. She had the oddest look on her face.

"What's wrong, Aggie?" Poppet plopped down beside her sister on the sagging bench and took her hand. "Are you ill?"

Aggie shook her head.

"Are you sure?" Niddie asked, standing in front of her sisters. "You're very pale. Do you need some water? You almost look liked you've seen a ghost or something."

Aggie straightened up and shook her head as if she needed to throw cobwebs out of her brain. "I, uhm, I think I might have." She sagged back down again. "What I just saw can't be possible though."

Poppet patted her hand and rubbed her fingers. "What did you see, for Heaven's sake?"

Aggie looked up at Niddie. She uttered in an astonished tone, "I swear I just saw Willie Mason, but he was only about 30 years old. Look! There he is!" She gestured toward the pot shop they'd been watching. A tall young man strode out of the door with a large package under his arm. Without hesitating, he turned toward them and walked up the other side of the street.

"Oh, my God," Niddie gasped. "If I hadn't seen him for myself, I'd have called you crazy and sent you to bed for being in the sun too long."

Poppet looked from sister to sister. "Who's Willie Mason?"

"Have you seen how many people have gone in there?" Niddie asked around the lip of the glass of iced tea she was lifting to her mouth. "We've sat here for over an hour and dozens of people entered in that short time."

Aggie nodded. She leaned toward Niddie and questioned, "Are you thinking what I'm thinking?"

Both sisters looked at Poppet who'd finished her sandwich and was working to get the last Oreo cookie crumbs from the bottom of the milkshake she had ordered. Slurping sounds came through the straw. Poppet was completely entertained and paying no attention to them at all.

Looking at her middle sister with a glint in her eye, Niddie continued, "I do believe so. Let's finish lunch. When we finish the shopping, we'll go sit by the pool and think this idea out. I think we may have a target."

Aggie shook her head. "Before we make a plan, we need to go inside and see what's in there." She lifted her sandwich for another bite. "You and Poppet finish up the shopping and take everything home. I already have everything I need. I want to go over there and see what's in that shop. When I come home, we'll talk about a Whoodah Thunket plan."

Niddie shook her head. "I'm not sure that's a good idea. We need to be together on this." Niddie smiled. "Besides you know how cranky she gets if she's left out."

Poppet burped and continued to slurp.

"I know," Aggie laughed, "but do you think we can go in there with ..." She jerked her thumb over her shoulder at Poppet who still wasn't paying a bit of attention to the conversation. "... the nun? And have her act inconspicuous?"

Niddie nodded in agreement. Aggie was right. Whoodah Thunket might approve, but Poppet would never be able to keep her cool.

Chapter Sixteen

The ladies stood on the marble steps of the impressive brick building overlooking the bay. Above the well-lit door was a fresco of an antelope head with the words, "To gather, to help, to serve ... friends of good will are always welcome here."

Poppet was unimpressed. "I don't know why I had to get dressed up and come here," she whined. "I could've stayed in the pool and you could've told me all about the place tomorrow." She tugged at the neckline of her dress and grimaced. "Clothes are just so confining."

Niddie rolled her eyes and Aggie snickered. "Get over yourself Poppet! Being in the pool alone is just not safe."

"Besides we need to be here together so we can all look around for an ... hmm ..." Aggie paused to think. "... an opportunity!"

Poppet harrumphed. Niddie grabbed her elbow and they walked into the great hall. Immediately, a tuxedoed gentleman stepped forward and stood before them. “I’m sorry, ladies. This is a private club. I’m afraid ...”

Indignantly, Niddie stepped forward. “We know this is a private club. We’re here visiting from out of town and we don’t know anyone in the area. We’re here as people of good will ...” She pointed to the sign.

The gentleman lifted a gloved hand to his lip to hide a smile and sniffed softly. “Ladies,” he stated. “I’m sure your people of very good will, but, first and foremost, this is a gentleman’s club. Ladies must be accompanied by a member or be the wife of a member.”

Aggie cleared her throat loudly and held out an elegant black card with embossed silver lettering. Immediately, the man’s demeanor changed. He barely looked at the card before returning the note to Aggie and bowed deeply over her hand.

“Welcome, Mrs. Hennenfent,” He looked beyond her and nodded at the other two. ”... and guests. “As the widow of an esteemed member, you’re always welcome here. Allow me to escort you to the small ballroom where dinner is now being served.”

Aggie smiled with grace and then looked over her shoulder at her surprised sisters. She lifted her chin haughtily, raised an eyebrow at them and then handed her wrap to the now deferential gentleman.

"That was an amazing meal," Niddie groaned softly as she leaned back and surveyed the room. "I could do this every night. The music. The lights. The service. Ooo, yes."

Aggie laughed and nodded agreement. "If we keep this up, we'll need strong young men and wheelchairs to get us back to the car!"

Poppet sniffed and stated, "Yes, this place would be perfect ... if only there was a pool."

An unobtrusive waiter stepped up behind Poppet and cleared his throat. "Pardon me, ma'am, but the small pool is just beyond that wall." He pointed to the distant end of the dazzling dining area. "You'll also find a complete spa and workout room there as well. Members only, of course. And the Olympic sized pool is on the other side of the club grounds."

Poppet's face lit up and she started to stand. The alert waiter grabbed her chair before the seat clattered to the ground. At the same moment, Niddie grabbed Poppet's arm and fiercely shook her head.

Poppet plopped back into the chair with a scowl on her face and muttered, "I just wanted to look."

"Can I bring you ladies anything else?" The waiter asked. Niddie shook her head. Aggie requested another glass of wine.

"I don't suppose you have any Oreos?" Poppet grumbled, but looked at the waiter hopefully.

The waiter tipped his head to the right and glided away from the table.

Niddie glared at Poppet. "You are a piece of work!"

Aggie cautioned her sister. "Don't start in on her now, Niddie. Let's not spoil this evening." She leaned forward. "Have you seen anyone who looks approachable?"

With one last warning glare at Poppet, Niddie faced Aggie and shook her head. "I see lots of wealthy people, but we need to find a way to talk to some of them." Aggie nodded. Poppet continued to slump in her chair.

At that moment, a tall, silver-haired gentleman appeared at Aggie's side. He was so handsome that even Poppet sat upright and took notice. "Excuse me, ladies. Which of you is Mrs. Hennenfent?"

Niddie looked at Aggie and Poppet pointed at her. The gentleman turned to Aggie, extended a hand and introduced himself. "I'm Marcus Garber. I'm the president of this club. Our maître d' told me that you were here. I came over to personally welcome you and ask if there was anything that I could do for you."

Poppet opened her mouth, but Niddie grabbed her arm again and squeezed before she could say anything.

Aggie extended her hand. "Why, thank you, Mr. Garber."

"Marcus, please," cooed the man as he bent over her hand.

"Thank you, Marcus," she smiled coyly. "I think we're fine. We're in town for a few weeks visiting my daughter who will be returning soon from a tour with Doctors Without Borders. Since we know no one else here, I thought a visit to this club which has always been so welcoming to guests would help us meet a few people."

"Well, then. Meet them you shall." He smiled down at her. "Let me introduce you to some of the members who are here tonight. I'm afraid the crowd is quite sparse as we have a large party planned for tomorrow night. You must be sure to come ... as my guest, of course." He looked up and scanned the room. "Would you like to dance? I see several people who probably worked in the same parts of the world your husband worked in. I can introduce you while we're on the floor."

Aggie looked at her sisters. They both motioned her to go ahead. Marcus smiled down at them. "Don't worry. I'll be back for you two." He winked. Poppet giggled and Niddie beamed as Marcus led Aggie to the elegantly lit dance floor.

Much later that night, once again ensconced beside the pool, Aggie gave a gentle satisfied sigh. "That was fun."

"Amazing. I haven't danced that much in a very long time." Niddie stared off at the stars over the ocean and listened to Poppet splash around in the pool. "And can you believe that waiter actually found Poppet some Oreos! The look on her face was priceless! What a great club!" Niddie turned her head to look at her sister. "We need to go back again. I met several potentially interesting people."

"I agree," Aggie sighed again. "Besides, with an invitation from the president himself, how can we not go to the gala event tomorrow? But, right this moment, all I want is a foot rub and a good night's sleep!"

Niddie laughed. "I can get you to your bed, but..." She yawned mightily. "... you're on your own for the foot rub!"

Chapter Seventeen

The following night the ladies returned to the club. They were shown to a second even more graciously appointed room.

"This is amazing," Poppet gasped, staring around at the opulent room. Where the room in which they had eaten in the night before had been romantically lit table by table, this room radiated light. The chandeliers glowed above the dance floor, putting off small darts of light as they turned gently. Pristine white table cloths lay under crystal candle holder and glasses, brightly polished silver, and gold-leaf china.

"I thought the room we were in last night was gorgeous." Niddie shook her head as she continued to gaze around in awe. "No wonder they called the other room the small ballroom!"

The same maître d' who'd greeted them the night before, now dressed in white, escorted them to a table near the dance floor. They had a perfect view of the entire room while they ate a meal that was fit for the queens they felt like they were.

"I could do this forever," sighed Aggie.

Niddie sniffed. "Not me. I enjoyed the smaller room, but this is all too much for me."

"I'd rather be in the pool," Poppet added. "I wonder if they'll have more Oreos."

Men in their finest tuxedos escorted ladies in silk and satin to and from the dance floor. Aggie pointed out, "Just sit and watch the people. We need to make a decision tonight."

"Look at that one," Poppet pointed a finger at a garishly gowned woman who danced on the edge of the crowded dance floor. "She kinda looks like a giant green peacock." Poppet lifted the elegant candlestick in the middle of their table. "Mrs. Peacock in the dining room with a candlestick." Niddie snickered behind her hand at the reference to their favorite childhood game.

"How about the man in the shiny bright blue suit?" Niddie answered. "Reminds me of a spring sky!" She leaned forward and whispered. "Maybe he has an axe!"

Poppet giggled and nodded. "Mr. Blue in the garden with an axe."

Niddie gestured toward the dance floor. "And look at our Aggie." Both women looked at their sister in the arms of a handsome gentleman. "She looks so happy."

Niddie had to admit that this was a side of her sister she'd never seen. She'd always known Aggie as the quiet middle sister who kept the peace in the family, but here under the golden lights and in this opulent situation, she looked very different. Her smile was bright, her mannerisms animated and elegant. She looked completely at ease with the wealthy company. Niddie had to shake her head several times in subtle astonishment.

"Wait!" Niddie grabbed Poppet's arm. "Look at that one?" She pointed casually to a man standing at the bar across the room. "Can it be ...?" Poppet's eyes followed Niddie's finger. "Is that ...? Naaaaww!"

"Who are you looking at?" Poppet saw the man and gasped.

Niddie nodded. There, leaning against the teak wood bar, chatting with the bartender, stood an old high school friend. "I'm not sure but that could be THE Willie Mason? The real one?"

"Aggie's old boyfriend? He sure looks like the one we saw in town but this one is much older."

Poppet's head bobbed like the toy dog in the back of a car window.

"What are we going to do?" Poppet breathed. "Should we get Aggie and leave? Are we going to tell her?"

"Why should we leave?"

"Niddie! Aggie said he broke her heart." Poppet exclaimed softly. "I don't know if she ever got over his leaving."

Niddie blew a raspberry. "Of course, she got over him. She married Jeremy and had a great life with two great kids. That is water long gone under an old, old bridge."

Niddie looked at her sister who was being guided around the edge of the floor, dangerously close to the ghost from her past. Niddie held her breath as she danced within inches of the man she'd dated all through high school. Everyone thought they'd marry and be together forever ... until his father had moved the family away in their junior year. Aggie'd been heartbroken. She wrote to Willie almost daily for months and lived for the days when one arrived from him. Gradually, his letters slowed down until they stopped completely.

"What is Aggie going to do?" Poppet asked.

"I don't know, but I think we need to at least give her a head's up," Niddie stood up just as her sister's dance partner twirled her face to face with the man from her past. Niddie had read about something happening that made the world stand still, but this was the first time she had ever actually seen the phenomenon happen. Aggie dropped her partner's hand. Willie straightened up and stared at his long-lost love for several moments.

Niddie blinked tears away as she watched them rush to each other, their joyous laughter ringing out above the music.

Poppet squealed happily, clapping her hands. Niddie sighed with relief and sat back down. "Looks like we aren't going to have to do anything."

They watched as Aggie turned, graciously thanked her dance partner and turned back to Willie. The world noises resumed and swirled around the two as they chatted. After several minutes, they linked arms and strolled toward the table. If Aggie'd been smiling before, now she glowed. Willie looked equally happy as he patted the hand Aggie had tucked into the crook of his arm.

"Look who I found!" Aggie laughed. Niddie and Poppet stood up and stepped around the table to greet Willie.

"Well, if it isn't Willie Mason! Please sit with us," Niddie invited him, indicating an empty chair. "Is anyone with you? We can make room."

Willie shook his head. "No, I'm here alone. But, please, I outgrew Willie years ago. Here everyone knows me as Liam. Much more dignified name, don't you think?" He sat back in his chair and looked around the table.

The three women looked at their old friend and smiled. Niddie said, "Well, I may forget once in a while, but I do think Liam fits you."

Poppet shook her head. "I don't get your nickname. Willie is short for William ... that I get, but where did Liam come ... OOOOOOH!!!" She nodded her head as the realization hit her. "Yes, that makes sense." Poppet held a hand out and smiled, "Nice to meet you ... Liam."

Liam took her hand and smiled. He turned to Aggie. "How about you? Can you come around to using that name?"

"Of course," Aggie grinned. "I rather like the change."

Liam surveyed the table once more. "I just can't believe you three are here. I never thought I'd see you again, let alone looking so gorgeous in an Antelope Club!"

Niddie blushed and looked down. Poppet beamed, dabbed at her lips with a napkin. Aggie laughed and leaned against Liam's arm.

"You sure haven't lost your gift of baloney, Liam."

"What baloney?" Liam put a pseudo-shocked look on his face and clapped a hand to his chest. "I just says 'em like I sees 'em, ma'am! I bet I'm the envy of all the males in the room. Three gorgeous women all to myself!"

The sisters couldn't resist the giggles that rose up. Liam lifted a hand to signal a waiter. Instantly, one appeared over his shoulder. "With permission, of course, I'll be joining these ladies." All three murmured consent. "Bring us a magnum of Dom Perignon Brut please and four glasses."

Poppet rose up slightly, "Oh, oh, only three glasses," she said.

Liam looked at her askance. Poppet dropped her eyes coquettishly and answered shyly, "I ... well, I became a nun ..."

"For two months ... years ago!" Niddie scoffed, not about to let Poppet try to fool another person.

Poppet glared at Niddie and then turned back to Liam. "Well maybe my time there was only two months long, but I still believe now what I believed then. I never drink or smoke or do anything a nun wouldn't do ..." She stopped for a second thinking about why they were there. "... except accidently."

Liam reached across the table and took Poppet's hand. "I'd never make you do anything against your beliefs, Miss Poppet. But this is truly a special time. I'll have them bring the glass and maybe you'll join us for a small sample. This is the best champagne in the world."

"Well," Poppet blushed and pulled her hand back.

Liam winked at her and then to Niddie before turning back to Aggie.

"I cannot believe you remembered," Aggie gasped in delight. Niddie and Poppet looked at each other. Liam smiled warmly and reached for her hand. He brought her fingers to his lips and, just before planting a kiss, told the other women.

"I once promised Aggie we'd drink the biggest bottle of the champagne named after her daddy as soon as we could legally buy one." He kissed the fingers and then whispered, "This celebration's been too long coming."

"The champagne is named after Daddy?" Poppet clapped her hands.

Niddie said, "The wine called Dom for short, Poppet."

"Oh, just like Poppa. Well then, of course, I'll drink to him," Poppet smiled. She waggled a finger. "But just a little sip or two."

Liam looked at the grinning Niddie. "No need to ask me twice. I love a good champagne."

Chapter Eighteen

Later, after a fine meal and four bottles of champagne, the little group sat reminiscing.

"What I don't understand is why you never came back to look for our Aggie," Poppet piped in after draining her third glass of champagne.

"Well, there were a lot of reasons." Liam signaled for the waiter, indicating he wanted another bottle of the fine wine brought to their table.

Aggie gasped and grabbed his arm. "Liam, are you sure? That's very expensive stuff."

Liam patted her hand and nodded. "I'm very sure."

Tipping his glass up for the last drop, Liam emptied the crystal stem wear and looked at Poppet to answer her question. "There are no good reasons. Basically, I was so mad at my father for moving us that I became a tough kid, getting in trouble all the time, angry at the world. Eventually

I ran away and joined the military. Then, life just sort of took over. I was determined to make a career and, when I had enough to make a good life with Aggie, I was going to come back." He paused for the waiter to fill the glasses again. He lifted the glass in salute. "Then I got hurt in Viet Nam. Landmines." All three women drew in sharp breaths.

Liam tipped his head. "I was a mess. No one thought I'd live but I did. Then they thought I'd never walk. I did. Then my attitude was so awful because of the pain and addiction to pills that I couldn't get a decent job."

"Where were you?" Niddie asked.

"Oooh, here. In this land of sunshine ... most of the time," Liam leveled his gaze at her and smiled ruefully. "This is really the best place to be a homeless vet."

Aggie's hands flew to cover her gasp. Poppet's eyes welled up. "Why didn't you contact us?" She asked sadly. "We never left our home. We'd have been glad to help."

Liam nodded. "I would've been grateful, but there were several good reasons to stay here. OK, first I didn't know if Aggie was still available. Then I'd heard you married."

Aggie nodded, mixed emotions playing on her face.

Liam asked, “You were happy?”

She nodded again. “Until he died several years ago.”

Liam kissed Aggie’s fingers again. “That I didn’t know.”

“Did you ever marry?” Niddie asked.

“No, I didn’t. Like I said, I was in a pretty bad place with the pain medications and alcohol. Of course, I had my share of women over the years but none could compare to our Aggie.” He lifted Aggie’s hand once more and kissed her knuckles. “But ...” Liam answered honestly. ”... I did have a son.”

He looked at Aggie, trying to judge her reaction. To her credit, Aggie just waited for the rest of the story. Pleased at the lack of shock on her face, Liam continued, “I was seeing a nurse for a while. When I started using again, I didn’t want to deal with her disappointment in me so I returned to the streets. I didn’t even know she’d had a child until he found me when he was 17. That was ten years ago.” Liam raised his glass in salute. “Eric made me get off the streets and I started to be a real person again. We’re actually in business together.”

"I'm so pleased to hear that," Aggie said. "So you're here now because of your work with your son."

"Sort of," he smiled. "Turns out between the two of us, we have quite a head for business. We own several small shops across the state." He took another sip from the glass. "But these days I'm pretty much a figure head. I go to parties ..." He gestured around. "... join fancy clubs and hobnob with people who might want to invest in our business."

"Very impressive," Niddie looked at him over her glass, feeling quite light headed. "Sort of rags to riches then."

Poppet, who was slumped slightly in her chair, tittered but said nothing.

Liam laughed softly and commented, "I think Miss Poppet may have liked the champagne a bit too much."

Aggie looked at her sagging sister and said, "So much for 'just a little sip'! We better get her home." She turned to Liam. "As much as I don't want to end this, this is the time to say good night."

"I don't either, but I have an idea ... if you three don't mind. How about I have my driver take you home?"

"Your driver?" gasped Niddie.

"Yeah," Liam said with a bit of chagrin. "I know it's sort of a prideful thing but having a limo and driver is so much easier than parking and all that. Besides ..." He tucked his thumbs under his lapels and pushed his chest out. "Having them is good for the old image!" He looked at the surprised women and then let his chest fall with a gust of laughter. "Anyway, he'll take you home and then, if you're available tomorrow evening, I'll have him come and pick you up. I want you to have dinner with my son and me. He needs to meet the woman I have talked about so much over the years." He smiled at Aggie and stared deeply into her eyes.

"Well, uhm, yes ..." Niddie broke the silence and stood up. "I think that'll work quite nicely. Aggie, come help me with Miss Sloshed here." She put a hand under Poppet's right arm. "The story she's going to make up to explain her hang over tomorrow should prove interesting."

Aggie and Liam stood. Liam sent a text message on his phone while Aggie helped get Poppet to her feet.

"Can I help ladies?" He asked chivalrously.

"No, we can get her to the door," Niddie groaned.

"The car will be at the door in a few seconds. I'll escort you out."

Chapter Nineteen

"Oh my," Poppet walked out of the hallway the next morning, hand over her eyes, stumbling slightly. "My head hurts."

Niddie went to the kitchen to make another pot of coffee.

"Come sit down," Aggie patted the couch next to her. Poppet dropped on the sofa and moaned slightly. Niddie came in and put a steaming cup into Poppet's hands.

"Yuck!" Poppet sniffed the cup. "I hate coffee." Niddie stopped her from handing back the cup.

"I put lots of chocolate milk in the cup so the coffee will taste much better. You're going to need this caffeine boost," Niddie encouraged her.

Poppet took a sip, wrinkled up her nose, and moaned again. "I may never go to the pool again."

Aggie looked at her sister. "The pool? Why not? You love the pool."

Poppet gently shook her head. "I must have gotten too much sun yesterday. I think I have sun poisoning."

"Sun poisoning?" Niddie laughed. "There's no such thing."

"Yes, there is!" Poppet cried out. Immediately, she put her free hand to her head. "Owwww! Owww!"

Aggie patted her shoulder and said, "No, dear. I don't think there is."

Poppet stood up gingerly. "I read about sun sickness on the internet. If you're in the sun too long, you get sick from the heat and get all dehydrated and stuff."

"Don't you think you'd be very sunburned if that happened?" asked Niddie.

Poppet looked at her arms and turned to look at her face in the mirror on the wall next to her.

"Hunney ..." Aggie cajoled softly. "You got plastered last night. You drank too much. We had to carry you to the car."

Niddie snickered, "Fewer people might have noticed if you hadn't been arguing about leaving because you hadn't gotten your Oreos yet."

Blushing furiously, Poppet whipped around and glared at the other two. "I ... I never ... I ... ooooohhhh."

"Oooohhhhh, yeah," Niddie laughed. "I gotta say I was a bit mortified at the time, but now the memory's a little funny. We were pulling you down the hall and you were demanding to see the chef. You kept insisting he had to be hiding the Oreos somewhere for himself."

Sobbing loudly, Poppet jumped out of her chair, raced down the hallway and disappeared.

Aggie shook her head. "Why do you have to torment her? Can't you just go along with her once in a while?"

"No, I can't. One of these days she's going to have to stop believing she's a nun." Niddie snapped. She plopped down in her chair and blew out a heavy sigh. "So, what are we going to do?"

Aggie shook her head. "To be honest with you, I was so stunned at seeing Liam that I forgot about everything. His story was something else."

"I know," Niddie said in wonder. "He was always such a positive go-getter in high school. I'm having a hard time thinking of him as a bad boy or doing drugs or even in the military."

The sound of a door closing and feet shuffling down the hall behind them stopped their conversation. Without saying a word, nose in the air, Poppet paraded by in her towel. She glared at her sisters daring them to make a comment.

Niddie whispered to Aggie, “Where’s her suit?”

Aggie shrugged and explained, “I guess she’s over her sun sickness!”

Niddie pretended shock. “Now I’ve seen it all.”

“I think she’s lost her mind.” Aggie added.

Niddie smiled and started to make a comment. Aggie grabbed her arm and shook her head. “I think we should go out and grab some sunshine, too. How about you, Sister?”

She rose and followed Poppet out to the pool. She stepped through the door just in time to see Poppet fall face first into the deepest water.

“OH! MY! Poppet!” Aggie raced to the deep end of the pool. Niddie skidded to a stop at the edge beside her. Poppet sat on the bottom of the pool, still as could be.

Neither Niddie nor Aggie could stifle the giggles that rolled to their lips. From that angle, with a swirl of bubbles and her winter white skin, Poppet looked like a huge popcorn ball that had sunk in the deep end. The two sisters watched for a moment. Poppet made no move to return to the surface. More bubbles rose as she wiggled around trying to stay on the bottom.

Without a word, Niddie jumped in and swam down to pull Poppet out. Aggie watched as Poppet threw her arms out and slapped Niddie away. The water roiled with air bubbles and disturbed water. A few seconds later, Niddie came to the surface with an arm around a sputtering Poppet.

"You fool!" Niddie gasped between breaths of air. "What are you trying to do? Drown us both? Stop fighting!"

Aggie knelt down and helped Niddie out, but, as soon as Niddie let go of her, Poppet moved out of reach. Aggie cried out, "Poppet! Give me your hand!"

"No! Leave me alone!" Poppet turned her back and began treading water just beyond reach.

"But Poppet, you almost drowned and then you almost drowned Niddie," Aggie screamed.

"No, I didn't. I tripped. That's all." Poppet sniffed. "And then I was just enjoying the silence at the bottom of the pool. That's all! I was just fine!"

Niddie rubbed her face with the towel Aggie handed her. "Admit it, Poppet. You're feeling so bad that you had your eyes closed and you fell into the pool. Then you were too embarrassed to come up for air."

"What I do in the pool is none of your bees wax!" Poppet ducked under the water and dog paddled to the other side of the pool.

"She's a real piece of work," Niddie sighed with a reluctant smile in her voice. She stood up and moved to the sun shelf in the pool. Aggie followed her. Sitting under the umbrella with her feet dangling in the water, she asked her sister again. "What should we do? We only have a couple weeks until the kids get home and then we won't be able to pull off anything without explanation."

"Well, I was thinking about one thing," Aggie muttered.

"And that would be ...?" Niddie looked at her sister with interest.

"Promise me you won't get upset," Aggie timidly requested.

Niddie threw the back of her hand to her forehead and mimicked a maiden in distress. "Me? Upset? Why I, ma'am, am the model of a calm woman and I'm distraught you'd think otherwise."

"Oh, give me a break," Aggie smiled at her sister's histrionics.

Niddie laughed out loud and asked, "So what's your idea?"

"Ok, but steady ..." Aggie sat down in the sun chair next to her sister's. "What if we tell Liam the problem and get his input?"

Niddie sat upright and roared, "Are you out of your mind?"

Aggie lifted her hands, palms out to quiet Niddie's tirade. Poppet turned at the sound. "I asked you not to over react. I don't mean tell him everything."

"And what part are you thinking of keeping from him? The part about how desperate we are or maybe the part about we're here planning to commit another crime?" Niddie stood and began pacing in the shallow water, arms on her hips. On the other side of the pool, Poppet slipped down in the water until only the top of her head from her nose up showed. She watched her sisters like a crocodile lurking in a lake, waiting for dinner.

"I know," Aggie said sadly. "Now that I've said the words out loud, I see too many problems."

"Ya think!" Niddie threw her arms up in the air and plopped back down in the chair. "If he didn't have us arrested, he'd think we were hitting him up for the money. We don't want either of those to happen."

Aggie stared at her lap and nodded. Seeing the sadness on her sister's face, Niddie reached out to put a hand on her arm. "You two just found each other again. Telling him about this would definitely put a damper on things, if not, end them all together and I know you don't want that."

"No, I was just grasping at straws," Aggie said.

Niddie sat back in her chair and watched a lone rain cloud slip along the horizon, long fingers of grey rain connected the cloud to the sea. "Let's just go to dinner and meet the son and see what happens. Maybe they'll let something slip. If not, we'll go back to the club sometime this week."

Chapter Twenty

Liam's driver knocked promptly at 7. When Poppet opened the door, he doffed his hat and, with a slight nod, greeted her with, "Good evening. I'm Robert Court. Mr. Liam sent me to gather you up and take you to his home." He smiled and looked Poppet in the eye. With a wink, he added, "I trust madam is feeling better today."

Poppet blushed. "I have no idea to what you refer. I'm fine as always." She sniffed in disgust and stepped back. "Please wait here." She closed the door and turned to see her snickering sisters. "I hope you're happy."

Aggie's eyebrows flew up. "Us? What? We didn't do anything?"

Niddie smiled and added, "We can't help that you can't hold your Dom Perignon!"

Poppet started toward the hallway. "I'm not going if I'm going to be ridiculed all night." She tried to shove her way between her sisters. They each grabbed an arm and walked her backwards toward the door.

"You're going," Aggie said. "You'd be rude not to go. Besides the only other person who knows what happened last night is Liam. He won't be hard on you. You might as well ride out the course of torment and get over the teasing."

Poppet shook off her sister's hands and turned to march to the door. "Let's go then." She put her chin up, pulled the door open and sailed through like a queen, pausing only to sniff indignantly at the driver as she passed him. Aggie smiled at him and shook her head, trying to let him know he should just ignore Poppet.

The trip took less than ten minutes. When the limo pulled into the drive, Aggie thought the road was a forgotten country lane. Tall palm trees bent over the cobblestone alleyway, making the ride feel like a trip down a magical path. The house didn't come into view for several seconds. When the building did appear, all three women gasped. The place they were staying in was huge and beautiful, but this one made their temporary home look like a hovel in a field.

"My good Heavens!" Poppet whispered under her breath.

"Indeed," answered Aggie. Niddie held her peace.

The car stopped and Robert turned to the back seat. "Quite a sight, isn't it? I usually stop here for a few seconds and let first time guests look for a bit. Tell me when you're ready to go."

Aggie leaned forward. "Liam lives in this whole place?"

"Well, the home actually belongs to his son. The main part is where young Mr. Mason lives. Mr. Liam has that one story wing on the left and the other side is usually unused unless long term guests are being entertained."

"Wow," Niddie finally added to the conversation.

Poppet leaned forward and whispered, "Is there a pool?"

Robert winked, "There are two ... one fresh and one salt water."

Poppet gasped. Niddie interjected, "You can drive on now. I think I see someone on the verandah."

The limo eased smoothly down the cobbled road. Along every inch of the drive stood a new discovery. There was a huge green leafy bush shaped like an elephant and another like a towering winged griffin. Iron statues of horses and soldiers were scattered around the manicured lawn. In the center of the lawn stood a white marble fountain with leaping dolphins spewing sparkling jewels of water in all directions. The delighted women pointed out each new work of art until the driver pulled to a stop under the marble portico at the front of the house.

Liam stood in the entryway, smiling broadly as the car came to a standstill. Robert jumped out of the front seat and ran around to open the door, but Liam was there to help the ladies out.

"Welcome to my little house," he said with a grand wave of his hand. He reached down and helped Niddie out of the back seat.

"Little?" Niddie gasped. "If this is little, I'd hate to see your idea of big."

Liam leaned down and extended a hand to Poppet.

"Both sheds, the barn and our house would fit nicely inside this place," Poppet proclaimed, looking around.

Turning to the car one last time, Liam took Aggie's hand.

"Hello you," he smiled, looking into her eyes as he pulled her to him. Aggie grinned and kissed him on his cheek.

"Don't mind them," Aggie laughed. "I don't let them off the farm very often."

Liam threw his head back and laughed. "Well, come on in, ladies. I'll give you the nickel tour."

Twenty minutes later, the four were seated on the shady porch near a man-made running waterfall. Birds darted in and out of the trees above them. Robert had brought a tray of iced tea to the table and put one in front of each person. When he served Poppet, he smiled brightly and said, "Let me know if you need anything else." He slipped his hand into his pocket, pulled his clenched fist out and then reached for Poppet's hand. With a wink, he covered her hand and then withdrew his before returning to the house.

Poppet looked down. In the palm of her hand lay one of the round black and white cookies she loved so much. Her first instinct was to throw the thing away in embarrassment. Then she saw a tiny note tucked under the edge of the Oreo that read "I love Oreos too."

Poppet smiled and looked at her sisters. They were both busy enjoying their surroundings too much to notice Poppet. She popped the Oreo in her mouth and chewed as quietly as possible. Looking toward the house, she saw Robert standing just inside the kitchen door, with a broad smile on his face. Without thinking, she smiled at him and then hid her face, embarrassed at her own brazenness. When Liam spoke, she turned her attention back to the conversation.

"My son should be here soon. I'm excited to have you meet him," Liam said. "You'll like him. I'd probably be six feet under if he hadn't come along."

"What do you mean?" Aggie asked.

"When I was discharged, I had a lot of healing left to do. The doctors gave me an unending prescription of oxycodone, a pat on the ass and sent me along. I was in a lot of pain, day and night." He took a deep swallow of his tea. "I couldn't get a job so I started taking more oxy and drinking to fill in the gaps. Pretty soon I was going through oxy so fast that the pharmacies refused to fill the script." Liam shook his head.

Aggie patted his arm and said, "I'm so sorry."

Liam shrugged. "I spent about five years out there, drunk or stoned or both." He shook his head. "I wouldn't wish that on anyone, but I did meet some great people out there who were on the street for a myriad of reasons. Most of them not even their fault. Then I met the lady, the nurse, I told you about."

Niddie's eyebrows raised. Liam continued. "She took me in and tried her best to get me off the drugs. She really made me want to try, but I just couldn't manage living without drugs. I was back out on the streets a couple months later."

Aggie sighed, "I was hoping she'd straightened you out."

Liam shrugged again. "I guess I wasn't ready. I wandered around for nearly twenty years. Sometimes I'd find a job. Then I could stay straight enough to do good work for a while and that felt great to be productive. Once I even had a house for almost six years, but I always fell off the straight and narrow."

Poppet leaned forward and asked, "So how did you get here? This is a long way from the streets."

"That's where Eric comes into the picture." Liam raised an arm and waved to the house. Robert stepped out of the shadows on to the patio. "Robby, bring us another round. Is Eric here yet?"

"He called and said he'd be about 10 minutes longer," Robert told him.

Liam nodded. "He's a great kid. He actually found out about me and searched for almost four years till he found me. He was the one who got me off the streets, cleaned up, and into his business. Even the name change was his idea." He winked at Poppet. "You have to admit Liam is a much better name for a dependable businessman than Willie." Poppet nodded.

"Uhm ... what business are you in, Liam?" asked Niddie.

Liam sighed and looked off to the horizon again. "I think I'd rather have him explain the details to you when he gets here. He's the brains. I'm just the front man, the glad hander."

"Glad hander?" queried Poppet.

"Yup," Liam stood and walked around the table to Poppet. He took her hand and smiled deeply. "I'm guy the makes you want to do business with me. I'm the diplomat that assures you investing in our product is far better than anyone else's." Poppet's other hand flew to her throat as she felt the full force of his charisma. "Someone once said that I'm the kind of guy who can call you all sorts of bad names and have you thanking me and smiling asking for more information." He dropped Poppet's hand and laughed. Turning back to the other ladies, he said, "Let's go inside. I see Robert signaling that dinner will be ready soon."

With a soft "oh my", Poppet stood up with her sisters. Aggie looked at her and smiled, "Are you OK?"

Poppet looked up with a silly half smile. "Believe it or not, my knees are a bit shaky."

Aggie laughed, "That's the Liam I remember."

As they entered the dining area of the patio, they heard the front door open and a younger man came striding down the hall. This time Aggie was the one who gasped. "Wow," she gasped, "that's amazing!"

"I know," whispered Liam in her ear. "Looking at him is like looking in a mirror that turns everything back forty years."

Poppet grabbed Niddie's arm and leaned in as close as she could. "That's him! The one we saw!"

Niddie snapped at her. "Shhhh! I see him! Be quiet."

Aggie could only shake her head. This younger man was the spitting image of a Liam she hadn't seen in so long. She looked back and forth between the two men.

"Hello, I'm Eric." He walked directly to Aggie. "I know! There is no denying parentage!" He laughed and bent over her hand. "Father has talked of nothing but you since he got home last night. I'd have recognized you anywhere." He turned to the other sisters.

"You must be Niddie, the eldest." Niddie nodded her head as she shook hands. He turned to Poppet and put his hands on his hips.

"You must be Poppet, the Oreo lover." Poppet blushed furiously. "Please," continued Eric, "don't be embarrassed. I have a desk drawer full of cookies in both of my offices. They're not Oreos but ..." Behind him, he heard his father clear his throat. Eric looked at him to see him subtly shaking his head. "... but they're just as addictive to me."

Poppet smiled shyly. Niddie interjected, "I don't know why you need your father to be the front man with your gift of gab."

"Hey, now," Liam laughed, "don't be talking me out of a job."

"You're right, Miss Niddie. I'm pretty good at the glad handing," Eric laughed, "but the difference between us is that he enjoys schmoozing people!"

Robert cleared his throat as he cleared the platter of crudité from the table. "Dinner will be ready soon."

Liam stood. "Well, that gives me time to take you on a brief tour of the grounds. Anyone interested?"

Poppet jumped to her feet. "Robert said you have a pool! Can I, uhm, we take a look?" Liam laughed and held out a hand to her.

Niddie stood and looked at Aggie and Eric. "I better go and make sure she doesn't decide to jump in!"

"I'll stay here with Eric. You two go ahead." As Niddie walked off, Aggie turned to face her host. "I just can't get over how much you look like your dad!"

Eric laughed. "I know I get that a lot. But, you know, he has come such a long way and is a really great guy. I guess I could remind people of worse things!"

Aggie nodded and whispered conspiratorially. "You know you almost gave me a heart attack the other day."

"How?" Eric asked, concern written all over his face. "I'm sure I didn't mean to."

With a wave of her hand, Aggie told him about how she'd seen him on the street. "I would've sworn on a stack of Bibles in court that you were your father from so very many years ago."

Eric took her hand and squeezed her fingers gently. "I wish I could tell you how happy he is to have found you. I know for a fact you're the love of his life. He actually called you the 'one who got away' the first day he told me about you!" Aggie blushed. "And he told me that ... don't tell him I told you this. He'd had a bit too much of the bubbly ... but he told me he used your birthday as any numerical code he needs ... just because he knew he'd never forget that day."

Aggie felt like a teenage girl who'd just heard that her secret crush liked her back. Before she could respond, the others sauntered back onto the lanai and Robert called out that dinner was on the way. Eric stood and reached out to Aggie. "May I escort you to the table, madam?"

Fluttering her eyelashes like a coy Southern deb, Aggie took his hand and said, "Why, kind sir, I'd be delighted."

Liam called out. "What's this? Moving in on my girl?"

"Might I point out, dear father," Eric stated. "You have a woman on each arm and you left this one alone!"

"Point taken," Liam smiled at Aggie.

"Oh my," Aggie exclaimed, "What a lovely table." She waited as Liam stood behind her and pulled out her chair. Niddie allowed Eric to hold her chair and Robert rushed to seat Poppet. Once everyone was seated and had food on their plates, Aggie started up the conversation again.

"So tell us about your business," Aggie said to Eric. "Seems like you must be doing well to have all this."

Liam cleared his throat. "Aggie, we're in the medical cannabis business."

"Cannabis? What does that mean?" Aggie looked mildly shocked.

Niddie sternly answered, "That's marijuana, Aggie."

Poppet choked on the olive she'd just popped into her mouth.

"Like those people we saw at the café?" she gasped, wiping her chin. "The young people? You get people stoned?" Poppet leapt to her feet.

"Oh for heaven's sake, Poppet! Sit down!" Niddie scoffed at her sister's reaction. "There's more than one kind of cannabis." She looked pointedly at her host. "Right, Liam?"

"She's right, Miss Poppet," Liam lifted his hands. "Please sit back down." Robert stepped forward and held the chair for Poppet as she reluctantly sat back down.

"Ladies, please, let me explain. Our cannabis is not the bad kind ... the kind you take to get high. This kind is used to help people with glaucoma and cancer and other diseases. The sale of this kind recently became legal and we opened a shop to sell the medicines made from cannabis. That's all we sell!" He looked from one face to another, ending with the scornful Poppet.

Eric snickered. “Getting into this business just seemed a logical progression to us, considering what we used to do.”

Liam gave his son a glare. “Come on, Dad. There’s no shame in what we used to do.”

Niddie’s eyebrows raised. “What did you ‘used to do’?”

Liam ran a hand over his face, dropped them to his lap and then looked directly at Niddie. “I used to deal on the streets to make money for food and alcohol.”

Once again Poppet gasped. Shc wanted to push away from the table and run but this was Liam, a guy they had known all their lives.

“Oooooh, you were ...” she dropped her voice to a bare whisper, ”... a drug dealer?”

Liam smiled with chagrin. “I guess so, but I never did the hard stuff. No heroin or cocaine or anything else. Just the weed.” He looked at Aggie. “What are you thinking, Aggie?”

“Well, I’m just not sure. I mean, how did you go from living on the streets and selling dope to living like this?”

Eric chimed in. “When I finally found dad, I coerced him into coming to live with me in my downtown apartment. I was a low-level MBA in a nowhere job. One night during tax season, I came home exhausted and stressed out. Dad pulled out some weed and got me to try a couple puffs."

"I just wanted to help him out a bit," Liam added. "He was so tired."

"I got up the next day and felt great. Rested and alert, ready to go. No hang over or anything." Eric explained. "I felt so much better than I previously did any morning after I'd have to have a few drinks to wind down." He looked at his father who nodded for him to continue.

"So, after a lot of planning and talking, I used my meager savings and we moved out to a place near here and started growing our own weed. Dad knew who to sell to and I did lots of research on how to grow the stuff." He threw his hands up. "The rest is history sort of. We sold a lot of weed and, when the sales became legal, we applied for a license and became a real store."

Niddie shook her head. "So now you grow and sell marijuana?"

"Growing and selling the actual weed is still illegal unless you have a license from the state," Liam said. "We buy our products from reputable companies and sell only to those with prescriptions. Everything's all above board and legal now."

Poppet sighed. "Well, that's a relief." The other two sisters relaxed a bit as well.

"She's right," added Aggie. "We heard about these shops from a waitress and watched one across the street from a café one day. In fact, that's where I saw you Eric, coming out of one. There were a lot of people going in and out of the place."

"A lot of people needed our help. One of the best things about the legalization is that good people who couldn't get the medicine any other way don't have to put themselves in danger of being arrested or being hurt by thugs anymore to get the help."

Niddie scoffed. "That waitress wasn't a fan. She said that anyone could go to a ..." She looked at Aggie. "... what did she call them?"

"Dr. Feel Good," Aggie answered.

"Yeah, that's right and then anyone could get a script." Niddie continued. "There were some young people at the restaurant who were obviously high. She said they pooled their products and had parties."

"Like everything," Eric said, "There are people who abuse the system. But most of the customers are good, law-biding folks who just need a little medical help."

Poppet shrugged. "I guess it's OK then if it's legal and helping people."

"And ..." Aggie continued, "... you don't do the illegal stuff anymore, right?"

Liam looked at Eric. Eric nodded and smiled. "Well ..." Liam said. "We do have some of the other stuff but not in the shops. We keep that mostly for our own use and for a few trusted friends."

Poppet sprang to her feet. "Oh! My! God! I've heard that you users put weed in food to get other people hooked! Oh! Oh!" Poppet began reeling backward. "I'm feeling the effects. I feel, uhm, oooooh ... I think I'm getting high!"

Robert, who'd been standing by the door during the conversation, stepped in behind her in case she fell. Poppet turned and saw him. She turned back and threw her hand to her forehead. With a loud moan, she fell back into his arms. Robert caught her with a soft groan and gently lowered her considerable bulk to the floor. Poppet lay there with her eyes closed. Robert patted her cheek gently.

Niddie snapped. "For heaven's sake, get up, Poppet! You're being an idiot."

Poppet opened one eye. "Don't you swear at me, Enid Grace!" She let Robert help her sit up. "Thank you," she whispered at him.

Liam walked over and helped her to her feet. "Niddie is right, Poppet. We'd never do that to you without your knowledge. And ..." He gestured toward the table, loaded with fresh fruit, vegetables and grilled chicken, "There's nothing there to which we could've the pot."

"Yes, there is!" Poppet squealed. "See! Right there!" Poppet pointed to the chicken breast on her plate. Using her fingernail, she flicked a piece of green leaf off the meat.

Robert stepped to her side again. "Excuse me, Miss Poppet. I made the chicken and that's just oregano." Poppet blushed at Robert's announcement.

Niddie and Aggie both rolled their eyes and the other men smiled broadly. "They look very much alike to the untrained eye," Robert said reassuring her as he pulled out her chair and indicated Poppet should sit. She slowly moved over to the chair and slid onto the leather seat.

Chapter Twenty-one

"We simply cannot do this!" Poppet stood with her arms folded tightly across her chest. Aggie sat quietly on the overstuffed sofa and looked out at the distant lights of a boat sailing over the dusky horizon.

"Aggie!" Poppet stepped over in front of her sister and demanded. "Surely, you can't be serious. You cannot think this is a good idea." Aggie didn't look up at Poppet. She just shrugged her shoulders and continued to look straight ahead. The view of her sister's floral robe was nowhere as intriguing as the distant boat.

Poppet sniffed loudly and went to a chair across the room. "You've truly lost your senses this time, Niddie. I mean completely!"

Niddie, ensconced like royalty on a deep winged back leather chair, sat unfazed by her sister's tantrum. "Do you have a better idea? I mean, we only have a week and a half until Christine gets home and then we won't be able to do what we have to – not WANT to but HAVE to – do, Poppet!" Niddie rose to her feet and paced the length of the room.

"Come on. What other ideas to you have? We go home in ten days. In fifteen days we have to have the money for that little weasel or we're going to be looking for a new home." She laughed a loud scoffing snort. "I can just see ten or fifteen little ugly cookie cutter houses, all exactly the same, where our house, barns and fields are now."

Poppet gasped. Niddie whirled on her. "What? You don't like that? How about a strip mall? Or a factory? Or a casino? Surely you didn't think he wanted the land for its charm?"

Tears eased out of Poppet's eyes at the idea of her home being torn down. She dropped her head in her hands and sobbed.

"Niddie, do you have to be so mean all the time?" Aggie scolded.

"No, I don't." Niddie sneered, "But someone has to be realistic and you sure aren't stepping up."

"I need my Oreos," Poppet jumped up and went to the kitchen.

"Make some tea while you're in there," Niddie demanded. She turned to look at Aggie. "So what do you think?"

"As much as I hate the idea of breaking into Liam's shop," Aggie answered, "I think we have to. I mean, we know where the shop is, they've offered to give us a tour tomorrow and ..." Aggie rubbed her hand over her face and sighed.

"And what?" Niddie encouraged.

Aggie looked Niddie square in the eye and said, "I think I may know what the password for the security system is."

"You what?" Niddie said in astonishment. "How? Who?? When?"

Aggie shook her head and told Niddie about her conversation with Eric while Liam had taken Poppet and Niddie on the garden tour before dinner. "Eric said Liam uses my birthday for many of his codes. If he's like most people, he's a creature of habit and doesn't like to change things."

"We just have to stay close to the guys when they're operating the pads and see if we can get a glimpse of the code." Niddie began pacing again. "Even one or two numbers will confirm if he uses Aggie's birthday or not. I'm willing to bet - if there's more than one pad - the code's the same on each one."

"You're probably right," Aggie said.

Niddie stopped in mid pace and walked over to sit beside Aggie. "You understand - if we do this - you'll probably never see him again?" Aggie's eyes glistened as she nodded. "Are you Ok with that?"

"I guess I have to be, don't I?" Niddie slipped a comforting arm around Aggie's shoulders and the sisters watched the distant ship lights disappear over the darkening horizon.

"I'm going to miss this," Aggie said, gesturing toward the vista, "But I really miss home."

"Me, too," Poppet chimed in. She came around the corner with a bag of Oreos cradled to her chest, crumbs on her chin.

"Stop talking with your mouth full. That's nasty. And where did you get those? I specifically told Johanna not to pick any up no matter how you begged."

Poppet sat down in the chair furthest from her sisters and clutched the bag tightly. She looked at the blue wrapper, blushed a little and whispered, "Robert gave them to me."

"Robert?" The other two chimed together.

"Yes," said Poppet haughtily. "I think he likes me and I know he likes Oreos too. Maybe HE wants to see me happy."

Niddie stood and took a step toward Poppet who, not wanting her Oreos taken away, jumped up and raced toward the kitchen. "I hear the teapot," Poppet cried. "I'll get the tea." She disappeared around the corner.

Shaking her head, Niddie groaned, "Great! Just what we need. Poppet has an enabler boyfriend."

"Oh Niddie, for Pete's sake. He can't be her boyfriend."

A sound from the doorway made Aggie look up. Poppet stood there with the teapot in one hand and the bag of Oreos barely hidden behind her back. "And just why not?"

Aggie knew she'd need to verbally tap dance to avoid another of Poppet's outbursts. "Oh, sweetie. I didn't mean you couldn't have a boyfriend. Of course, you COULD have one. I'm thinking that this just isn't a good time considering with what we're planning to do and how soon we're going home." Poppet stared at Aggie with narrowed eyes for a few seconds and then seemed to accept her thinking. Poppet held up the teapot. "I forgot to ask what kind of tea you wanted."

The next morning the women sat on the lanai, soaking up the sunshine and finalizing their plan.

"So we all know what to do, right?" Niddie queried.

Poppet sniffed. "Yes, General, you've made us tell you a dozen times!' She sipped her freshly squeezed orange juice and then added. "I still cannot believe we're going to do this to poor Liam."

Niddie's forehead creased as she opened her mouth to speak, but Aggie stopped her. "Let's not have that discussion again. When we get there, Niddie, you'll take the lead and ask as many innocent questions as you can. Poppet will stick with Robert and I'll stay near Liam. We'll let them take us through the store and make sure we get a tour of the back room. Poppet, you're going to have to use the bathroom just before we leave so Robert doesn't notice us trying to see the codes."

"I know, I know, even if I don't have to," Poppet sniffed.

"Right," Niddie agreed. "And you need to make sure Robert shows you where the loo is."

Poppet whined. "But I really don't want him standing outside the door, you know ..." she blushed furiously and whispered, "... listening to what I'm doing."

Niddie grabbed her head with both hands. "Oh Jesus, Mary and Joseph, Poppet! You aren't going to be DOING anything. And why in God's name would he want to listen?"

"Enid Grace!" Poppet raised up to her full height and glared at Niddie. "You stop that cursing right now or I'm not doing one more thing." She turned her back on her sister and looked toward the heavens.

"Fine, I'm sorry. Do you hear me? I said I'm sorry," Niddie apologized but with a heavy hint of sarcasm in her tone.

Poppet turned back around with a self-righteous look on her face. "Don't apologize to me." She pointed up and, raising one eyebrow, glared knowingly. "Apologize to..."

Niddie sat down, deflated. "Fine! I've had enough. I can't win this. I'm tired of the fighting. Let's just forget the plan, enjoy the rest of the time here and then just go home and give up."

Poppet looked at Aggie who shook her head in order to make Poppet not say anything more. "We'll make this happen, Niddie. Don't worry. You know we always ended up working together and everything turns out fine." She patted her sister's arm. "The limo will be here in an hour. We need to get ready."

Chapter Twenty-two

Once in the shop, Niddie and Aggie followed Liam around closely as he explained all the odd and, to the women, unique things in the shop. The plain tan walls in the front sales area were loaded with shelves full of glass jars in a wide variety of shapes.

Clear jars with exotic sounding names– Black Beauty, FaceWreck Haze, Buddha's Sister, Atomic Northern Lights –filled the wide shelves along the walls behind the well stocked display cases. On one side of the shop, the glass counters showcased edible products from gummy bears to whole cakes, from hard candies to huge lollipops and cobalt blue bottles of oils in a myriad of sizes. Display racks in the center held things labeled bongs and pipes of all sorts of shapes and sizes, some odd-shaped things called grinders and smoke cans and even huge multi-armed glass and tube things called hookahs.

Niddie felt like a small child in a sweet shop full of the strangest candies in the world. Overwhelmed by the variety of items and equipment, she forgot to ask questions, but fortunately Aggie had hung on Liam's arm and every word that came out of his mouth. Even Poppet seemed focused as she wandered around the shop with Robert in tow.

Time to get to the business at hand. Niddie cleared her throat softly to get Poppet's attention. No response from Poppet.

"Ahem," Niddie cleared her throat a bit louder. Still no reaction. Slightly miffed, Niddie put her hand over her mouth and began to cough. Across the room, Poppet's head flew up as she remembered the cue.

"Are you okay?" asked Liam, walking toward her. Niddie waved him off.

"Sorry, just a little something in my throat." She glared at Poppet.

Aggie took Liam's arm and began to turn him back to the cases. Niddie glared harder at Poppet and tilted her head slightly toward the back door. Poppet glared back, stuck her neck out and mouthed "Fine!"

"Uhm, Liam, I hate to ask this but ..." Poppet walked toward him. "... do you have a powder room here?"

"Of course, let's go to the back. I'll show you where the bathroom is. Step this way." Liam walked to the end of the counter with Niddie and Aggie close behind and turned toward the back of the shop. He stopped at a plain door mark 'No Exit', lifted his hand to the security pad on the wall and then looked back at the ladies. "Would you mind stepping back a bit? I have to punch in the code."

Both Niddie and Aggie mumbled, stepped back a small step and half turned to look at each other. When Liam lifted his arm to punch in the code, Poppet pointed to one of the shelves behind her and asked Robert what a particularly odd-looking item might be. Niddie and Aggie continued to look at each other, chatting about what they'd seen, but from the corner of their eyes both tried to get a glimpse of even part of the code.

"There," Liam said with a satisfied sigh. "I don't always get that thing right the first time!" He pushed the door open with a swoop of his arm and let the ladies inside. "Step inside, ladies. Welcome to where we do the real work."

Long metal tables stood in the middle of a stark room. Stacks of bowls and pots and pans stood at the ready near the tables. Knives, scrapers, scales, and other cleaning and measuring tools stood in perfect condition ready to be used. White, wax-coated boxes marked with the names they'd seen out in the front were stacked on the neat metal shelves.

"Wow, it's so clean back here," Aggie looked around the room, craning her neck to take in everything.

"The room has to be clean all the time. This is where we do all the prep. There are sneaky inspectors who come around unannounced to be sure we keep everything clean and healthy. On these tables we clean all the plants of stems and seeds and make sure our customers only pay for usable product." Liam gestured to the far corner. "We even have a professional baker who comes in to create our edibles." All three women gasped at the beautiful baking area.

"Wow, I'd sure like to have a kitchen like that at home," Aggie smiled.

"A lot of cooks would," Liam responded. "We wanted the best so we can put out top quality. People know we take extra care to do things the right way here. We have a reputation of producing a top-notch product."

He turned toward Poppet and held a hand out. "Let me show you the ladies' room."

Poppet grabbed Robert's arm. "I don't want to take you from your tour duties. Those two are far more interested in kitchens than I am. I'm sure Robert can show me." Robert grinned and patted Poppet's hand.

"Sure. Go ahead Robert." Liam nodded. "And we're nearly done here. When you get back, will you go get the car? We'll leave from the back so no one thinks we're open for business."

Poppet and Robert walked to the other side of the prep area and disappeared into the shadows between the storage shelves. Aggie returned to Liam's side. "This has been fascinating. How many people do you have working for you?"

As Liam answered, Niddie wandered toward a door marked office. Noting there was no security pad by the door, she moved on toward the back door. The pad glowed brightly in the corner. She stepped back into the middle of the room and looked around. "Liam, I saw the cameras out front but I don't see any back here. Aren't you worried about people stealing from you?"

"Good question, Niddie. No, I'm not," Liam said sternly. "When I hire some one, we screen them carefully and then let them know that there will be no second chance if they're caught. They will go to jail." Liam stiffened up to full height. "I do my angry Viet Nam vet routine on them and so far we have been lucky."

"So no one's even tried?" Aggie asked.

"They may have been tempted but so far we haven't caught any one. I do have to say, several of our employees have medical scripts and they get their scripts filled at a deep discount. So the benefit of working here is much better than getting caught."

"I can see that," whispered Niddie. "Impressive." At that moment, Poppet and Robert sauntered out from the corridor between stacks.

"I'll go get the car, sir," Robert said formally. He lifted Poppet's hand and kissed her knuckles. Poppet blushed furiously and giggled.

"If you don't mind," she smiled coquettishly, "I'd like to go with Robert."

"Of course," Liam and Aggie agreed at the same time. They stood and watched the two walk toward the door. Poppet snuggled up to Robert's arm as he reached up and disarmed the pad. Then the two stepped out into the night air.

"Well then," Liam smiled down at Aggie. "Love seems to be in the air." Aggie looked up at Liam and smiled as sweetly as she could. Her heart constricted at the idea of what they were about to do to him.

"Seems you may be right," she sighed.

Niddie walked past Liam and Aggie and said, "We better get out there before something crazy happens between the nun and the chauffeur." She laughed out loud at her joke and took up a place by the back door.

Chapter Twenty-three

"OK, so now what?" Poppet whispered to her sisters as they hunkered behind the dumpster in the alley that ran at the back of Liam's shop.

"Whatever we're going to do," gasped Aggie. "Let's get moving. This place stinks."

With that, Niddie stepped out from behind the huge filthy green metal bin. Looking up and down the alley, she wandered several steps toward the shop before waving her sisters to follow her. Aggie and Poppet slipped out of the shadows and joined Niddie in the recesses of the shop's rear entry. A small sign announced the name of the shop and warned of security.

On the sign the words *Best Buds* stood out in bold block letters. Below that was a picture of a well-armed, but scruffy Viet Nam era warrior. The rest of the sign proclaimed *Protected by Colt, Glock and an angry owner. Enter at your own risk.*

Niddie smiled at the sign, remembering the night before during the after-hours tour when Liam told them how he'd made that up one night when he and Eric were quite stoned. They liked the idea so much they posted the warning both on the front and back doors as well as several places inside.

Beside the cash register, in clear view of all customers, were several photographs of Liam when he was in Viet Nam. He stood tall and glared at the camera, looking as seedy and dangerous as the protection sign intimated the owner of this shop would be. So far, Liam had confided, those signs and the pictures had deterred anyone from trying to break in.

Amongst the three of them, the sisters figured out the code was indeed Aggie's birthday like Eric said. Niddie reached up and pressed the numbers into the pad. Immediately the disarmed light came on. The three women stepped into the cool back room.

"Let's get this over with. I'm going to the office. Aggie, you watch the front but stay out of sight!" Niddie commanded. "Poppet! You watch the back and don't touch anything."

Poppet sniffed at the accusatory sound of her sister's command. "I won't. I said I wouldn't and I won't!" She watched her sister walk to the office door. She knelt down and pulled out her father's ancient lock picking kit. In seconds Niddie had the door opened. Hand on hip, Poppet watched. Niddie used the door handle to stand up and then slipped inside.

Poppet sniffed again and tried not to think about what her sister was doing in there. She wandered toward the kitchen and ran her gloved hand along the smooth metal table top. She admired the sparkling equipment that dangled from the heavy metal ceiling mounted pot rack above the long table. As she moved slowly, she counted the number of ladles and spoons that hung with the pots. Shaking her head, she wondered who would even need that many ladles.

Several tall metal cabinets stood at the end of the table. The doors looked like the corrugated metal on the barn roof at home. Poppet reached out to touch one. To her surprise, the metal was slightly warm even through the glove. Quickly checking to see if Niddie had come out yet, Poppet reached over to the latch and lifted the slide.

Immediately the delicious aroma of fresh baked brownies wafted out. Her nose twitched and her stomach contracted slightly. This was just unfair, she thought looking at the row after row of beautiful brown chunks of heaven. They'd eaten hours ago and she was hungry. She reached out her hand. Maybe just a taste of one little brownie wouldn't hurt anything.

Almost immediately, she heard Niddie's voice in her head. "Don't touch anything." She pulled her hand back as if her fingers had been burned. Poppet stood there looking at the gorgeous little squares. She reached out a hand again and pinched off the corner of the nearest one. Surely one little bite wouldn't hurt.

Poppet slipped the morsel into her mouth. Immediately, the soft, silky dessert dissolved on her tongue. She almost gasped out loud. That brownie was the best thing she'd ever tasted in her life. Even better than her beloved Oreos. *Niddie was just going to have to get over her anger,* she thought.

Poppet reached in and grabbed the rest of the brownie and took a huge bite. Oh, good heavens, she groaned, licked her lips and then her fingers. The taste of the chocolate warmed her entire soul. She closed the door and leaned against the metal. Eyes closed she sighed and did everything she could to get every drop of flavor out of the brownie crumbs in her mouth. She stood against the warm cabinet for a few minutes more, just enjoying the taste.

She felt an odd grin spread across her face. There was no reason why she should be smiling so broadly but she just couldn't seem to stop the feeling. Her whole body felt relaxed and happy. Suddenly, she wasn't scared or even worried about what they were doing here. More than anything, she just wanted to pull the tray of brownies into her lap and sit and enjoy them all. But she couldn't do that. Her sisters would be so angry.

With the flavor gone, she stood up and started to saunter away. But that chocolate was so good that she couldn't walk away. She hadn't been this happy for a long time. She turned back and stared at the cabinet. Her hand reached out as if the appendage had a mind of its own. Poppet smiled as she watched her fingers open the cabinet and reach in.

"Poppet!" At the sound of her sister's voice, Poppet gasped, jumped and closed the door. She leaned against the cabinet, trying to hide the evidence. "What did you do?" Aggie accused, pointing to a dark smear near Poppet's lower lip.

Giggling, Poppet lifted a finger to her lips and tried to shush her sister, but her teeth felt wobbly. Smiling at the idea that her teeth were as relaxed as she was, Poppet lifted her hand and used her hooked forefinger to beckon her sister closer. Slowly, she turned and opened the door enough to let Aggie see inside. She watched as the heavenly smell made Aggie's nostrils twitch. Poppet waggled her fingers at the delectable morsels and quickly closed the door.

Aggie put her hand on Poppet's shoulder. "Are those what I think they are?"

"They are incredible brownies."

Aggie reached around her sister and pulled the latch up. When she saw what was inside and the empty space, she whipped her head toward her sister. "Poppet! Did you eat one?"

Poppet's grin spread even wider. She nodded like a little bobble head dog in the back of a car window. She laughed at that idea and kept nodding her head until she saw Aggie start to shut the door.

"NOOOOOOO! You gotta try one." Poppet yelled and stopped Aggie from closing the door. She reached in and grabbed another brownie. "You gotta!"

Aggie shook her head vigorously. "They probably have marijuana in them."

Poppet looked shocked for a second. Then she looked at her fingers, laughed out loud, and shoved half of another brownie in her mouth. "Who cares," she mumbled. "They're amazing."

Poppet held the other half of the brownie up in front of Aggie's disapproving face and waved the innocent food around. The smell wafted up Aggie's nose, tempting her to take a small bite, but she held firm.

"Come on, Aggie," whispered Poppet. "You know you want to. Besides what harm will one little bite do? This one's already half gone. I can't put this brownie back." She moved the brownie like a snake charmer's pipe. Aggie's eyes followed the brown treasure. Poppet lifted her eyebrows in askance.

After several seconds, Aggie gave in and took the brownie from Poppet's fingers. She pinched off an end and set the tidbit on the end of her tongue. The instant the flavor of the treat hit her mouth, she stood stock still. That WAS the best thing she'd ever eaten in her life. Poppet stood there, grinning and nodding her head. "Told ya." she whispered.

Aggie reached in and gently took another brownie. "Niddie is gonna kill us." Poppet nodded and laughed out loud around the third brownie she'd just stuffed in to her waiting mouth. She grabbed one more in each hand and slid to the floor, leaving the door slightly ajar. "Sit here." Poppet patted the floor. "She'll never find us here." Aggie giggled, sat down and ate her second brownie.

The sisters sat there for long minutes looking at the gorgeous array of equipment and admiring the way the chocolate crumbs looked on Poppet's white shirt. They were in the middle of laughing at the crumb shaped like Niddie when their sister came rushing around the corner.

"What are you two doing?" She snapped. "We need to leave now."

"Shhhhh," Poppet put a hand up to her lips and shushed her. "Be quiet. You'll wake the brownies." Poppet pointed to the open door of the cabinet across from them. Aggie fell against Poppet and the two giggled in each other's arms.

Niddie didn't laugh. "Oh my God! What in the world have you two done?" She looked into the cabinet and counted six empty spaces. Behind her, the two sisters, still giggling, struggled to help each other up off the floor. Between their laughing and their lack of coordination, the task took several minutes and attempts to accomplish.

A disgusted Niddie stood, hands on hips, in stunned silence. *How in the world are we going to get out of here now*, she wondered.

Poppet finally stood upright and pointed to the cabinet. "You gotta try one! You just gotta. Right, Aggie?" She turned toward Aggie so quickly she almost fell again. Aggie caught Poppet and steadied her as best she could. "Doesn't she, Aggie? She's just gotta." Aggie nodded. Poppet lifted her hand and showed Niddie a brownie.

Aggie looked at her stern sister and said, "Sister." Niddie turned toward her. "You need this."

Poppet tapped her shoulder and, when Niddie opened her mouth to argue, pressed the warm brownie in. Aggie and Poppet loosed gales of laughter at the shocked look on Niddie's face and collapsed on the floor again while Niddie swiped at her chin and spat.

Aggie looked up at her sister's angry face but couldn't keep from laughing. "Oooooo man," she moaned to Poppet. "She's gonna kill us for sure this time."

Poppet howled with laughter and rolled against her sister. "Not if we can get her to eat a couple more."

The hysterical women slid further down into a laughing heap at Niddie's feet. Niddie had to admit that brownie was good, but she didn't have time for this. She alone was going to have to figure out how to get them out of here. She looked at that quivering pile of sisters on the floor and sank down beside them. There was really nothing to do but to let the dose run its course.

She noticed another crumb of brownie on her hand and lifted her finger to her lips. By her count, each sister had eaten at least three brownies. From what little she knew about marijuana, the effects could last a while. She licked her finger again and thought *that is good. Maybe I'll have just one.*

An hour later, Niddie woke up. She felt a silly smile spreading on her face. She had to admit the effects of that brownie were still in her system and felt pretty good. But they had to get out of here. She began to coax her sleeping sisters into waking up.

Aggie stirred first, yawning and stretching. "How long have we been asleep?" she asked. "That's got to be the best nap I've ever taken." She looked around and realized where they were.

She looked at Niddie who nodded. "We should've been out of here hours ago."

Niddie tried to snarl but gave a lopsided grin instead. "I know that. How do you feel?"

Aggie took stock of her body. Her eyebrows lifted. "Surprisingly well, but I'm not sure about her." Smiling at the memory of her giggling sister, Aggie realized she might still be slightly high, but Niddie didn't need to know that. She looked at the still sleeping Poppet. "She ate more than I did."

Niddie nudged Poppet's shoulder. Poppet groaned and slapped at her. "Leave me alone," she muttered.

"Fine," Niddie said, "but we're leaving. You'll be here alone in a minute or two."

Poppet's eyes flew open and she looked around. "Why are we still here on the floor?"

"Because you couldn't contain yourself," Niddie scoffed.

Poppet smiled broadly, "Oh yeah." She pushed herself up and extended a hand out to Aggie. Helping her sister to her feet, the two looked into each other's eyes and began giggling again. This time, to their surprise, Niddie joined them while moving then toward the door.

Poppet insisted on visiting the restroom first. Niddie put an arm around each sister and walked them toward the bathroom, working hard not to stumble into another heap on the floor. When they reached their goal, Poppet stepped inside.

Almost immediately, they heard her gasp and call out to them.

"Aggie! Niddie! Look! Come here!"

Aggie followed Niddie to where Poppet stood in front of a long mirror just outside the bathroom, still giggling like a little kid. Poppet grabbed Aggie's arm and pulled her in close to her. She pointed at the warped mirror and said, "Look at this!"

The mirror threw back a distorted image of the room and its occupants. "I'm ..." Poppet threw her arms out and then dropped her right hand to her hip and lifted her left hand into a graceful curve. "... a teapot." The children's song raced through Aggie's mind as she stared at her snickering sister.

Slowly, she felt waves of laughter rising up in her abdomen. Poppet grabbed her arm again and, barely able to speak, said, "And ... ha ha ... look at Niddie! Ha ha ha!" She fell against Aggie. "She looks like a long tall spoon."

That was the last straw for Aggie. She looked at Niddie who was staring into the mirror with a blank expression on her face. The gales of laughter Aggie felt rising burst out, "I guess that makes me the napkin!"

At that, all three sisters burst into laughter and leaned against each other. Tears began pouring out of all three sets of eyes as they tottered but tried to stay upright. Aggie felt her legs began to weaken. She knew her knees were about to give out.

"Uh, oh," she laughed. "Here we go again!"

Another louder burst of laughter filled the air as the three women slid into a pile against the mirrored wall. They lay laughing, weeping and gasping for air until they were too weak to move. Niddie felt a warm glow laying there with her sisters. The last time they'd snuggled up together had been so long ago. Her eyelids grew heavy. Somewhere in the deepest part of her mind, Niddie knew they should get up and go home. But this was just so comfortable, this warm, happy pile of sisters.

"We're gonna need more of these brownies," she whispered to the room and drifted off.

Chapter Twenty-four

"What in the hell do we have here?"

Niddie jerked awake at the sound of Liam's voice. She looked up to see his scowling face. Eric and Robert looked disapprovingly over his shoulder.

Niddie scrambled to her feet. "I ... I can explain." She reached out a foot and nudged Aggie. Aggie groaned and opened one eye. As soon as she saw the men, she woke up and got awkwardly to her feet. Sleeping on the floor was not something her body approved of any longer. She pushed Poppet's shoulder and urged her awake. Poppet muttered and grumbled but rolled over. Shock clouded her face when she looked up. She held out a hand to Aggie.

"Help me up." She struggled to her feet. "Liam! Eric! Robert! What are you doing here?"

"I'd ask the same of you," Robert snarled. "I must say this is a very disappointing thing."

"I can explain," Poppet stepped toward him but Niddie reached out a hand to stop her. She stretched her neck up and stiffened her back.

"We can explain ourselves." She looked each man in the eye. "But we're not going to do it now. Robert. You're going to take us home. We're going to clean up. Eric and Liam, we'll come to your place at noon and give you a complete explanation. But that's all you're getting now." Once again, she scanned the faces, defying the men to object to her demands.

After a few long seconds, Liam stepped up. He took Aggie by the arm and guided her toward the back door. "You better get out of here before the others show up."

"Liam, I ..." Aggie started. Niddie put a hand on her shoulder but Liam beat Niddie to the warning.

"Not now, Aggie," Liam growled. "I need to decide if I'm angry, hurt or just disappointed. You three need to leave." He turned his back on the women. "Robert! Drive them home! Now!"

The women shuffled out the back door and into the limo. Robert slammed the door behind them and strode to the front. He slid into the car without a glance into the backseat. Not speaking a word, he drove the women through the barely lit alley.

Aggie looked out the back of the limo and saw Liam standing in the shadows. His head was hung. Eric's arm was around his father's shoulder. The sorrow that Aggie felt ripped through her and brought tears to her heart.

The sisters sat around their kitchen table, each with a cup in front of them. The last time they had sat around this table seemed like a lifetime ago.

"What are we going to do?" Aggie sniffed.

"I don't know." On the other side of the rickety old table, Niddie put her head down on her arms.

Poppet walked over to her sobbing sister. Niddie never cried. Poppet was unnerved to see her in such a state. "Don't cry, Niddie. We did the right thing. I'm proud of us for not taking the money Liam and Eric offered. I just hope they'll forgive us for leaving without saying goodbye."

"Me too," Aggie sniffed.

Niddie lifted her head and wiped the tears away. "These are just happy tears. I was thinking about last night."

Just after dinner, a solid rap on the front door had made the women jump. "Who do you think that might be?" Aggie asked Niddie.

Poppet's face darkened. "You don't think that might be Robert? Or Liam!" She pushed out her chair and walked to the door. The other two remained in their chairs, not as optimistic as their younger sister. They heard Poppet's voice and then a deeper male voice answered. Aggie looked at Niddie and her brow knit. "You don't suppose ..."

Both women shifted in their chairs and waited. When Poppet came around the corner, a tall, lanky man followed her into the room, but not the man either of them hoped to see.

"Good evening, ladies," Frank Moore doffed his hat and made a shallow bow in their direction. Niddie's heart skipped a beat despite her sorrow. *The Marlboro man*, she thought. A brief moment of brightness was followed by the thought of what she was sure he wanted. Niddie let her brow furrow.

"Oh for Pete's sake, what do you want?" Niddie snarled as she turned back to the table. "I still don't want to talk to you. And besides how did you even know we were back?"

"Dougie, the cab driver, told me you were home."

"Dougie!" scoffed Niddie. "He never could keep his mouth closed."

"I know about your problems, ma'am," Frank said softly, "Geena at the library told me the basics."

Niddie stood up fast enough to knock her chair over. "Why can't people keep their noses out of other people's business? If I'd wanted the world to know our problems, I'd have taken out an ad in the paper!" Frank moved behind Niddie and picked up her fallen chair.

Frank held her chair while she sat down and then continued, "But I do have something of great importance to tell you. I cannot ... or rather ... will not put this off any longer. I either sit here and tell you now or I wait on the porch for as long as you take to give in and talk to me." There was only a short pause.

"Fine, sit down. You're giving me a crick in my neck staring up at you." Niddie groused. "Poppet, get this man a cup of coffee please."

Poppet moved to the stove as Frank sauntered around to an empty chair and sat down. *The very size of him makes the kitchen feel even smaller*, Niddie thought. She refused to let the look of him lighten her mood. She sat back, arms crossed and glared at him.

"Look. We're going through a very hard time right now. State your piece and move on. But you might as well know, we're never going to sell this place to you willingly."

"Sell? I'm not here to buy your place."

Niddie looked at Aggie. Both women looked back at Frank with eyebrows raised.

Aggie said, "Then why on Earth are you here?"

"I've been trying to tell you." Frank pulled a packet of papers out of the inside pocket of his jacket and laid the sheaf on the table. He waited for one of them to pick up the papers. Neither woman moved. Frank placed his long fingers on the edge of the packet and pushed the pages toward Niddie. "You really need to look at this."

Niddie snatched the pages off the table with a disgusted sniff and lifted the reading glasses that dangled from a chain around her neck. She took a long moment to settle them halfway down her nose. Before she turned her attention to the papers, she looked over the edge of her glasses with her most disdainful look as if to say this better be worth my time.

To his credit, she noted, Frank's smile never wavered. He held his ground despite her best effort. She opened the pages. Across the top were the words Purchase of Mineral Rights.

"Purchase of rights?" Niddie looked over the top of the pages at Aggie. Poppet slipped up behind Niddie and Aggie came around to Niddie's side of the table. The three women read the words. The pages slipped onto the table as Niddie's fingers loosen their hold.

Frank broadened his smile and leaned back in his chair. "See? This is important."

Aggie said, "I see the words, but what exactly do they mean?"

"Yeah," Poppet glared at the man. "Just what does this mean? What do you want?"

Frank held his hands up to calm the storm he felt rising in the women. "Ladies, this is what I have been trying to tell you. Several weeks ago, my company did a mineral search of your land."

Niddie jumped up. "You came on our land without permission?" She pointed to the door and ordered, "Get out!"

"No," Frank continued, hands out as if pushing the air between them down to calm the tone, "no one came on your property. With new technology, we can examine beneath the surface for miles from a central place. That's what the explosions are that you have been hearing. Oh and while I'm on that topic, the company's more than willing to reimburse you for the eggs your hens didn't lay, the milk your cow withheld and any other problems we may have caused."

Poppet sniffed. "Well, at least that's something." Aggie nodded.

Niddie continued, "So we sign these papers and we get reimbursed?"

"No." Frank said matter-of-factly. "You get reimbursed for that no matter what." He pulled a check out of his other jacket pocket and laid the paper on the table. He looked into the sad face of each woman. "No, if you sign these ... well, you become, uhm, very wealthy women." He waited to see the light of understanding come into their eyes.

"Wh-wh-wh-what?" Aggie stammered. Niddie reached out and grabbed her arm. Poppet leaned on Aggie and waited.

"We found valuable minerals under your land. We want the right to go in and retrieve them." Before they could ask, Frank said, "With new technology and mining techniques, there will be little if any damage to your land. In fact, you'll hardly know we're here."

Poppet gasped. “Ohmigod! Ohmigod! Niddie! Aggie! All my prayers are answered! Finally!”

The three women stood and wrapped their arms around each other, sobbing in happiness. Frank watched them and felt the emotions rolling off them. “I hate to intrude ladies, but someone needs to sign these papers.”

Aggie’s cell phone rang. She picked up the case from the table and her face brightened further. “This is Liam. I think I’ll answer the call this time.”

Poppet cried out, “I’m gonna call Robert!”

Moments later, Frank and Niddie were alone in the kitchen. Niddie looked at him sheepishly, “I guess I could’ve saved myself a lot of worry if I hadn’t been so stiff-necked.”

Frank smiled and handed her a pen. “It just so happens I like stiff-necked women.”

Chapter Twenty-five

The following morning, Frank drove to the farm. Liam and Robert had arrived early that morning and were sitting down to a lunch on the porch with the sisters. Niddie introduced the men and invited Frank to join them. They'd just begun to eat when a dust cloud rose near the end of the dirt road.

"Now, who could that be?" Poppet nodded. They all watched as the dust cloud morphed into a long black limousine.

Aggie gasped. Poppet stood and raced into the house. Niddie rose and put her napkin on the table. She looked at the concerned men. "Gentlemen, if you will give me a few moments. I have some unpleasant business to take care of."

Frank stood followed by Liam and Robert. "Can we help?"

"No, this is my fight. Just give me a moment." The men watched as Niddie smoothed her shirt and, followed by Aggie, walked down the stairs to wait on the sidewalk. Poppet emerged from the house with a grim look on her face and an old broom clutched in her white-knuckled hands. She strode past the men to join her sisters.

Liam put his napkin on the table and stepped beside Frank. "This ought to be interesting."

The driver raced around the car and pulled open the back door. The self-important young man stepped out and stood with his hands on his lapels while the driver used a small brush to swipe dust off his suit. Niddie struggled not to laugh at the kid's comical attempt at arrogance.

When he looked up, a shocked looked passed quickly over the young man's face. He pointed at Poppet. "You keep that crazy woman away from me, you hear?"

Aggie snickered. "What do you want Sactman? You're interrupting our meal."

Sactman pointed a finger and yelled, "You know why I'm here."

Frank cleared his throat, stepped onto the top step and warned, "You'll keep a civil tongue, young man, or you'll leave." He felt Liam and Robert step into rank behind him.

Sactman sneered up at the three men standing with arms crossed, glaring down at him. He looked away from the men and back to Niddie. "Ah, so you brought back up. Well, don't think you'll get out of giving me what you owe me. The law's on my side and you know it."

"Really?" Niddie stepped one step closer. "And you've talked to the sheriff, have you?"

Sactman cleared his throat and coughed, trying to maintain the tough guy façade. "Not yet but when I do ..." He started to shake his finger at her again but thought the better of it.

Frank walked over to stand next to Niddie. He looked down his long nose at the little man who seemed to shrink slightly. He looked back at Niddie. "Is this the one you told me about?"

Niddie simply nodded. Frank smiled and reached into his jacket pocket.

Sactman took an involuntary step back and fell against the driver who had turned several shades of pale. He pulled himself upright, tugged his lapels once again and, without taking his eyes off Frank, growled out of the corner of his mouth at the driver, "Start the car."

Frank pulled a long cream-colored envelope from inside his jacket. He extended the paper toward the barely steady young man. "Take it."

Sactman stepped just close enough to grab the envelope. Quick as a striking rattlesnake, Frank grabbed his wrist and squeezed. He pulled the trembling young man up close and snarled, "These ladies have recently come into a great deal of money. What's in that envelope will pay your so-called bill in full and some for your, uhm, trouble. If you ever step on this property or insult one of them again, I will personally have you thrown in jail for a very long time." He gave the wrist another squeeze. "Do you understand?"

Sactman cleared his throat again and tried to answer. Unable to form the words, he nodded. Frank dropped his arm.

The two stood glaring at each other for a long moment. Poppet, who had crept up behind Frank during the confrontation, stepped around him and stood in front of the frozen bill collector. She raised up her broom and yelled, "You heard him."

Sactman gasped and fell backwards, his feet scrambling to carry him out of harm's way, his mouth gaping like a fish out of water. He slipped and skidded his way to the car without turning his back on the wild woman with the weapon. As he pulled the door closed, they heard him scream, "Drive, dammit! Get me out of here."

A great dust cloud covered the car racing down the dirt road as the three couples burst into gales of laughter.

"Well," Aggie sighed, "That was fun."

Poppet sniffed. "I think it would have been more fun to bop him with this broom a couple times."

Robert laughed and put an arm around her shoulders. "Our valiant warrior woman!"

Chapter Twenty-six

Eighteen months later, six identical rocking chairs moved back and forth in perfectly synchronized movements. The sun was hanging low over the hills and beginning to tinge the sky with orange and pink. A fresh breeze wafted by, carrying the scent of lavender and roses.

Niddie felt Frank squeeze her fingers. "How are you? Doing ok?"

Niddie smiled. "I'm fine, though I think I'll be much better when this wedding is over."

Aggie quipped in. "Oh, me too. I'm already exhausted and we still have two weeks to go. Do you think the houses will be ready by then?"

Poppet laughed and smiled at the man holding her hand. "Mine will be!" She gestured at the old farmhouse behind her. "Our house just needed one room added ... one with a heated pool!"

Robert laughed and kissed her hand. "I have heard interesting stories about heated pools."

Liam snickered. "At first, I didn't know why you women insisted on these places being done before the wedding." He lifted Aggie's hand to his lips and smiled, "But I totally understand now."

Frank looked across at the rest of the people on the porch. "Come on. This town is geared up for its first ever triple wedding. The party's going to go on for days. Friends and family are coming from everywhere. We'll need space for everyone." He smiled. "Besides, we can't be expected to spend all three honeymoons in this little house now, can we?"

Niddie laughed and said, "Not the way Poppet swims!"

Ripples of laughter rolled over the porch into the valley as the sun sank further below the horizon.

And there you have the short happy life of Whoodah Thunket! I've decided to retire since I see no future need for me. The girls are taken care of for life ... just like Poppa wanted. Neither Niddie nor Poppet had any children and Aggie's progeny are stable in their own careers.

In light of their new found wealth and at the vehement demands of their youngest sister, the Bradentons received an anonymous cashier's check in the exact amount that was stolen from their safe. No one ever found out where the payment came from.

The general was pleased to find a special delivery package on his front step one fine morning. Inside were the rough-cut diamonds he didn't even know were missing. Well, he was pleased for the short time it took him to realize they were his own diamonds.

I doubt I'll ever hear another person say they need to go visit with good ole Whoodah Thunket. Unless ... well, let's just say while I don't condone crime, I'm always here for a chat. Give me a call. I'll be glad to sit down with you and help with any problem you might have. Until then ...

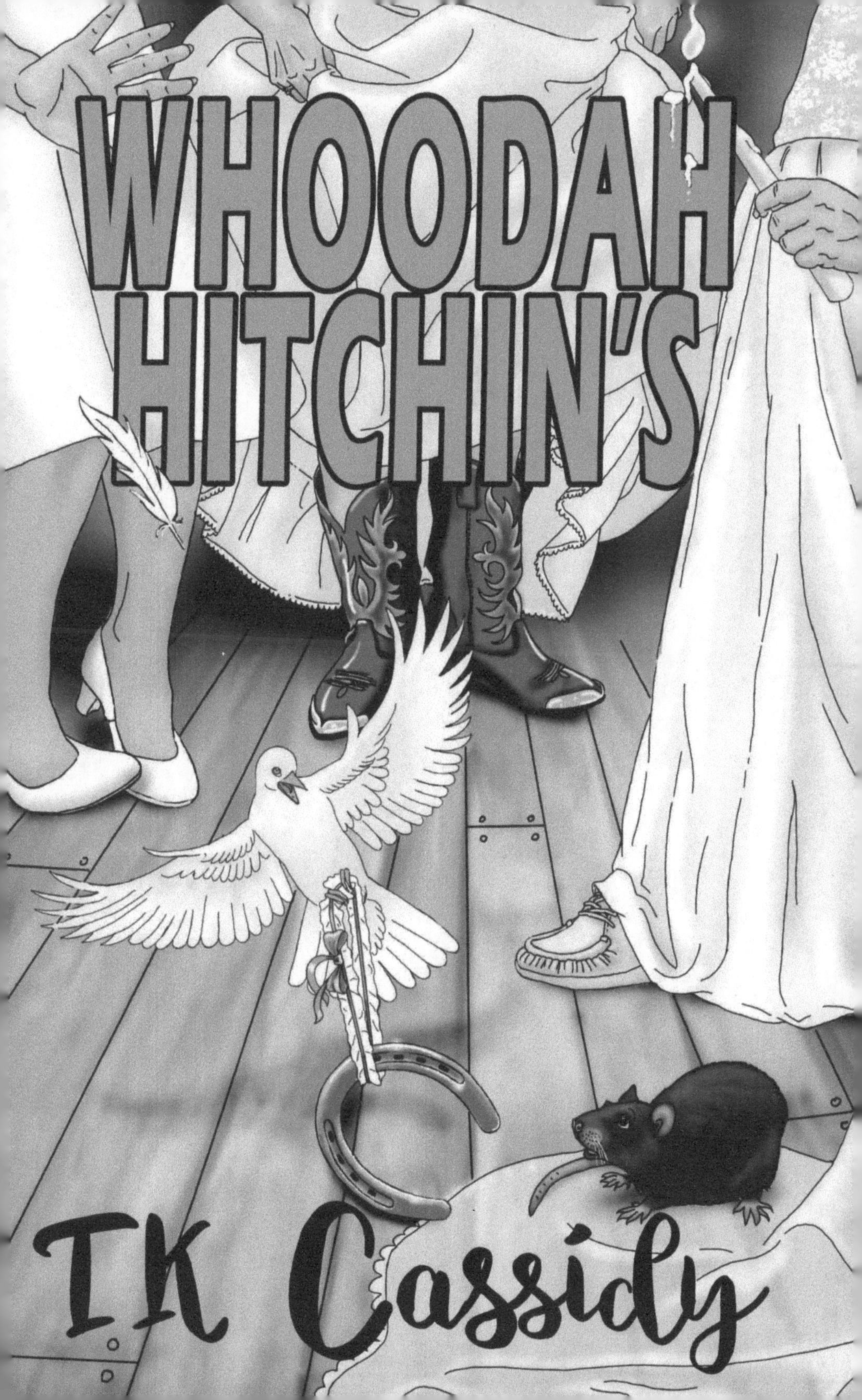
WHOODAH
HITCHIN'S
TK Cassidy

We're gettin' hitched!!

And you are invited.

Friday – 6 PM

Niddie and Frank invite you to their newly built barn for a hitchin' and a hoedown.

Judge Martin Osborne - officiating

Saturday – 4 PM

Aggie and Liam invite you to the main house for an informal wedding followed by a garden buffet dinner

Reverend James O'Malley – officiating

Sunday – 4 PM

Poppet and Robert invite you to the marriage rites in their newly built stone cottage.

Father James O'Malley – officiating

Come for one! Stay for all!

NO GIFTS PLEASE.

Donations can be made to local public and school libraries

Chapter One - Whoodah Hitchin's

The sisters stood on the newly paved circular drive overlooking the yellow tape and stakes that indicated where each new home – the barndominium as Niddie called her new house, the cute stone mini castle Poppet demanded, and the remodeled old homestead Aggie decided on – would stand. On this fine spring morning, the work of building two new homes and remodeling the other would begin ... if only ...

Without warning, birds lifted from the trees as harsh words exploded in the pastoral morning.

"I will NOT have a stone monstrosity in my front yard!" Niddie bellowed at her youngest sister. At 5'10", she had to bend over to go nose-to-nose with 4' 11" Poppet, but, despite her aching back, she was willing to do that to get her point across.

"And you think I want to look at a mini barn from my front window? Ha!" Vertically challenged Poppet didn't let Niddie's loud voice deter her. She rose up on her tiptoes, hands on her hips, and yelled back. "I have a right to my own house. You chose your design without needing or even asking my approval. Aggie just decided to remodel the house we grew up in ... without asking me. I should get to choose a style that favors me too! Without your approval!"

"There's more at play here than just what you want!" A derisive snort escaped Niddie's lips. "Think about it, Poppet!" Niddie shouted her down. "If I have the barn-shaped house which we have already started on, Aggie has the wood house which is already built and you want a stone cottage that looks like a church, what will we have?"

Poppet stared at the vein pulsing in Niddie's neck, puckered her lips and shrugged. She looked at Aggie who made a wry face and shook her head in confusion. They looked back at their tall bristling sister. She offered, "A bunch of houses that reflect our personalities?"

Niddie stomped a few steps away. Within half a yard, she whirled around and strode back. She glared at her sisters and put her left hand with three fingers extended in the air right in their faces. She touched her right forefinger to her left one and said in a soft growl, "Barns equal straw!" She nodded her head sharply and raised her eyebrows. Both sisters shrugged.

"I can see that." Aggie said to Poppet.

Poppet shrugged again. "So?" She pulled an Oreo cookie out of her pocket. Picking imaginary lint off the edge, she popped the cookie into her mouth. She chewed softly while waiting for Niddie to continue.

"You and those cussed cookies!" Niddie scolded.

Poppet glared, chewed harder and pulled another out of her jacket.

Exasperated, Niddie continued. She moved her right forefinger to her middle finger on her left hand. "Wood equals sticks! Huh? Huh? Wood to rebuild the old house!"

Again, neither sister reacted.

Flustered and red-faced, Niddie gasped. She touched her ring finger. "Cottage made of stone! Stone! Do you get it now?"

She waited for her sisters to grasp what she was trying to say.

"Oh, my stars and garters! Explaining things to you two is sometimes like watching ducks paddling through plaster! Look!" She touched her fore-finger to her other fingers again, one at a time, as she said the words louder. "Straw! Wood! Stone!"

When neither of them said anything, Niddie cried out, "Oh, for cryin' in a bucket! You don't see it! Three little pigs! We'll be the dad-blamed three little pigs!" Frustration oozed from every inch of her.

There was a brief moment of silence as the two younger sisters stared at their glowering older sibling. Poppet was the first to burst out laughing. Aggie coughed and turned away, trying to smother the chuckles that rose up.

Barely able to contain her anger, Niddie hands flapped in the air like a pair of caged birds. "I don't believe you two!" She rubbed a hand over her forehead. "You think it's funny! I can just hear it all over town ... 'those crazy Masterson girls! Just look at what they are doing now!' Unbelievable!"

Ever the peacekeeper, Aggie recomposed herself first. She walked over to Niddie and put an arm around her. "Dearie, calm down. No one will think of that except you. You are so much cleverer than most people. You have always been too worried about what other people think. And who cares anyway?"

Poppet pulled another Oreo from her pocket and popped the whole thing between her lips. As soon as she could talk again, she interjected,

"Aggie's right. Calm down. I can see that big vein pulsing in your neck! You're going to give yourself apple ... uh, apop ... uhm, app..." Her face clouded over as she tried to remember the word her mother used when someone was too angry. When the word apoplexy would not come to her, she pulled up a different word and smiled, "a stroke!"

Aggie walked Niddie over to Poppet.

"Poppet. Stop."

"She started it!" Poppet wiped an escaped crumb from her lips and then dusted off her hands. "What a silly thing to worry about."

Niddie shrugged off Aggie's arm and shook her finger at Poppet. "It's not foolish. Just because you don't mind being seen as a doddering old goose ..."

"Oh, farfinpoopin!" Poppet cried.

Aggie stepped in once more. "Stop it, you two. No more arguing. We're going to settle this without screaming like fishwives – inside please. Look around you."

Across the circular drive stood three men in coveralls and boots, leaning against a King cab truck, watching the melee. Behind them stood bigger trucks full of wood and building materials along with construction equipment and workers with a variety of skills ... some standing, some squatting, some leaning against the equipment. All of them waiting patiently to start working.

Aggie waggled her fingers at the three closest men and smiled broadly. Niddie and Poppet followed suit. Their husbands waved back. Aggie continued, "All those workers are standing there watching three foolish old women bicker about who can have what kind of house. They cannot start until we stop arguing. And they are costing us a fortune! Let's go inside and discuss this."

As Aggie herded her sisters toward the original farmhouse, the men looked at each other.

"Do you think it will always be like this?" Frank Moore, retired engineer who had fallen in love again with Niddie, his childhood sweetheart, queried. He stood with his back side against the front quarter panel of his truck as they watched the conflict. He had tipped his hat down over his eyes and crossed his booted feet at the ankles.

Liam Mason, retired entrepreneur and current project manager, stared down at the topographical map spread out on the hood of the truck. The property had been clearly marked.

Everything was ready to go ... except the final decision on what was being built. He let a gentle snort slip out. “Yup. Only thing is ... as much as I love Aggie ... I don’t remember signing up for the bickering.”

From the front seat of the cab, Robert Court, CFO for this massive project, watched his wife, Poppet, and the other women walk toward the old farmhouse. “Yeah, you did!”

The other two men looked at him from under the bills of their hats. Arched eyebrows silently asked for clarification. Robert heaved a resigned sigh. “My brothers, when we said ‘I do’, we agreed to everything!”

The three men let loose a collective sigh. There was no denying the truth in that statement. They loved their difficult ladies dearly but, when an argument broke out, they had learned stepping aside and waiting until the dust settled was the safest course of action.

Now, if the women could just finish deciding they could get to work. Shaking their heads, the men turned and began giving orders for the sedentary crews to begin the resurrection of the old barn.

About the Author

TK Cassidy started writing at the age of seven. Her first novel took twenty-four years to write while life led her through thirty-eight of the fifty United States and placed her in Australia and Guam for a time.

TK has a Bachelors in English & Library Science, a Masters in Library Science and a Doctorate in Virtual Education. She worked as a children's librarian for twenty-five years.

While in Guam, TK authored over one-hundred-and-fifty children's stories as a columnist for a local magazine, for which she was the recipient of Guam's Maga Lahi award (named for the ancient Chieftain of the Chamorro). Her best-known story, *Dolphin, Dolphin* ushered her into becoming a travelling storyteller nicknamed 'Dolphin Lady', traversing

Guam and the surrounding islands before returning to the United States.

Since retirement, she's turned out one novel per year, edits for several authors and is an active member of the Tuscaloosa Writers and Illustrators Guild.

For more check out https://tkcassidywrites.com